Sunkissed

Happy Reading!

Leigha Lennox

By
Leigha Lennox

Sunkissed

2nd Edition
Printed in the United States of America.

ISBN-13: 978-1511775380
ISBN-10: 1511775386

Publisher: Traci Hohenstein
Tracihohenstein@gmail.com

Cover design by Pam Kennedy
Editing by Janet Fix
Interior book design by Bob Houston eBook Formatting

For Nikki Campbell

Thank you for all the years of friendship and laughter

Chapter One

Trista Carmichael carefully applied her lipstick and gave one last look in the rearview mirror before getting out of her gleaming, white Mercedes coup. Today was an important day. She was meeting a network executive about her contract renewal on the hit TV show, *You Only Live Once*. Trista was the star of the popular nighttime comedy show, which was about a girl who has a near death experience. Her character, Molly McBride, realizes, after coming back from the brink of death, that life is too short, and she sets out to complete a bucket list. The show was in its third season, and Trista had already won numerous awards for her role in the series.

Trista turned her keys over to the valet and waltzed into the Polo Lounge. Being a major star in a hit TV show definitely had its perks. The maître' de recognized her as soon as she walked in, and she was ushered straight to a table where Gil Salmon was waiting. As usual, the table was located in a prime area of the posh restaurant. Several male patrons discreetly watched as Trista sashayed through the crowded establishment.

"Trista, you look lovely today," Gil greeted her.

Trista had taken special care to look her best for this luncheon. She'd bought a new Dolce & Gabana dress the day before. It was a beautiful, white A-line dress showed off her perfect California tan. She'd also spent the morning getting her hair and makeup professionally done. Her long, blonde hair cascaded down the small of her back in beautiful waves, and her makeup had been applied with the precision only a trained makeup artist could pull off. Trista was known for her "natural beauty," which really took the right bronzer, fiber mascara, and tinted lip balm to achieve. Trista knew by all the subtle stares she looked like a million bucks today.

"Thanks, Gil," Trista said, planting a light peck on his cheek. She took the seat across the table from him. The waiter magically appeared to take her drink order and promptly left.

"How's everything going with you?" he asked. "Any special plans this weekend?" Gil was in his late forties. He had thinning, red hair, which he tried desperately to cover up with hair transplants, and a chubby face complete with wire spectacles. Trista knew Gil was also on his second wife, having dumped his starter wife when he got a promotion at the studio.

You Only Live Once was on hiatus for the next few weeks. Most of the crew took this time to go on vacations and relax until the show started filming again. However, Trista never stopped working. She usually had some type of work lined up, like commercials, voice-over work, or special appearances. Trista was fearful if she stopped working, or even took a break, all her work would dry up, and then she would have to move back home. The thought of being a "has-been" terrified her.

"Everything is wonderful. I'm taking a girl's trip with Quinn to a spa in Arizona this weekend. Afterwards, I have the photo shoot for Vogue. I'm up for a voice in the new Disney movie too." Trista noticed

Gil's raised eyebrow and quickly added, "Although it won't interfere with our show."

Gil took a sip of his water. He stared at Trista for a few uncomfortable seconds. The look made her stomach lurch. "I think some time off would do you some good. You've worked very hard for this network, and the show has gotten some fantastic ratings over the years. I know we don't tell you as often as we should, but we really appreciate your dedication." Gil paused as the waiter brought over a basket of breadsticks and Trista's iced tea. He told the waiter to hold on a few more minutes before taking their lunch order.

Trista felt dizzy with excitement. *Here it comes*. He was going to offer her a new contract. She wondered how much money he was going to throw at her. Right now, she was the highest-paid actress on the show. She made a hundred grand an episode. It was over a million-dollar payday. Per season. Her co-stars made less than half of what she did, and she knew there was a little resentment because of it. However, she was the big star of the show, and in her mind, that justified the higher salary.

"...that's why it is difficult for me to tell you this." Gil paused, clearing his throat. "We've decided not to renew your contract."

Trista's smile disappeared from her face. She suddenly felt sick to her stomach. "What? I don't think I heard you right."

Gil reached over to touch her hand. "This wasn't an easy decision, but the network thinks we need to shake things up a bit next season. Our ratings are still good, but we're competing against some excellent shows this fall. We've decided to take the show in a new direction."

"But what about my character? You can't do this! I'm the star of the show. The glue that holds everything together!" Trista tried to keep the desperation out of her voice. She looked around to see if anyone was staring at her.

"Your character will be killed off," Gil said matter-of-factly.

Trista stared at him in disbelief. "How?"

"Molly dies while skydiving in Europe."

Trista tried to digest everything he was telling her, but it didn't make sense. How could they keep the show going without the main character?

"You can't do this," she repeated. "Molly *is* the center of show!" Trista felt like she was going to puke. "*I am* the show. You can't go on with *You Only Live Once* without me!"

Gil waved off the waiter, who was heading in their direction. The waiter saw the commotion and whirled around, away from their table. "You're causing a scene, Trista. Calm down."

"How can I calm down? You're telling me I'm out of a job? A job I've had for over three years? I don't understand how a successful TV show can go on without their biggest star?" Trista tried hard to stem the tears that were threatening to flow down her perfectly made-up face. Dabbing her eyes with a napkin, she snuck a quick peek around the restaurant again to see if anyone had noticed her meltdown. They had. Everyone was definitely staring now.

"I'm sorry, doll. But the decision is final." Gil pulled out a wad of cash and put it on the table. "I'm afraid I have another meeting, but please stay and order lunch. It's on me. Good luck with the Disney thing."

Trista watched as Gil sauntered out of the restaurant, pausing at a couple of tables to say hello to other diners. She couldn't believe it. The last three years of her life, she had given all she had to the show, and now she was being fired. What was she going to do now?

Chapter Two

Trista decided not to wait until evening to tell Blake about her dismissal from the show. She knew the news would spread like wildfire throughout Hollywood, and she wanted to be the one to tell her fiancé. He was going to be very pissed when he found out Gil Salmon had fired her. But he would know exactly what to do. Blake Simmons was not only her fiancé but her agent as well. He was THE agent to the stars in Hollywood. Blake represented some of the biggest names in TV and movies. He was also handsome, charming, and well connected. If anyone could get Trista another big role, Blake could.

Before she could go to his office, she needed to freshen up. Her makeup from this morning was now ruined, and she wanted to change into something more comfortable. They had been living together for over six months and had recently become engaged. Blake wanted them to move from her condo into something bigger. So Trista put her West Hollywood condo on the market, and they had been looking at houses closer to the studio. Now Trista had been fired, she supposed they would put the house hunting on hold for a while. No sense in buying anything until she figured out what to do next. With her popularity on the show, she was certain she would land another spot on a TV series fairly quickly. Or maybe Blake could talk to Gil and work something out.

Trista pulled into the parking garage and noticed a green BMW parked in her space. It looked like her real estate agent's car. Blake's black Range Rover was parked in his spot as well. She must have forgotten the condo was being shown this afternoon. It was just as well. She could now tell the agent face-to-face she should take the condo off the market.

She entered the elevator and punched in the special code that took her directly to the penthouse level. As soon as she got off the elevator, she noticed the front door was ajar. A pair of bright-red heels was left in the foyer. Trista put her purse down on the console table and walked to the living room. It was empty. "Hello?" she called out. *The real estate agent must be showing the unit to a prospective buyer.* She wondered if Blake was with them.

She checked the guest bedroom and the kitchen. Both were empty. She opened the door to the master bedroom. Also empty. That's when she heard a sound coming from the balcony. Her condo had great views of Hollywood and the San Gabriel mountains. It was a major selling point and the real estate agent liked to take clients outside on the spacious balcony to show them the sights. When she'd first listed the condo, the real estate agent also recommended Trista spend some money making the balcony more inviting. Taking her advice, Trista had recently installed a new hot tub, bought new patio furniture, and added a lot of potted plants. She eased the sliding glass door open, but a large potted palm blocked her view of the hot tub. However, Trista could clearly see clothing scattered about the steps leading to the Jacuzzi.

Her stomach tightened, and she felt sick…again. The voices were a little clearer as she got closer to the Jacuzzi. Trista rounded the corner to see the backside of her real estate agent on top of her fiancé. She was riding him like a Shetland pony at a kid's birthday party.

"Blake?" Trista called out as she stood on the top stair of the Jacuzzi, where she had a full view of the sexual act going on.

Blake had his face planted firmly in the large breasts of the real estate agent. He looked up at the sound of Trista's voice, pushing the real estate agent off of him and standing up. Droplets of water cascaded down his nude body and off his huge erect penis. "Trista! What are you doing home? I thought…I thought…you're supposed to be having lunch with Gil."

"It didn't go so well," Trista couldn't think of anything else to say. For the second time today she was caught off guard. Stunned.

The real estate agent, a petite Asian woman named Cherie, stepped out of the tub. She grabbed a towel from the edge of the Jacuzzi to cover her oversized, fake boobs, picked up her discarded dress, and hastily made her way inside the condo without saying a word.

"Jesus, Trista. I'm sorry." Blake stood there in all his naked glory. Trista reached over and threw him the other towel that had fallen from a nearby chair. She wasn't sure if he was apologizing for fucking around or for the lousy lunch she had. "What happened at lunch?"

Trista felt numb all over. She couldn't think straight. Her voice sounded robotic. She answered, "Gil said they were moving the show in a different direction…"

Blake wrapped the towel around his waist and walked over to her. As he tried to put his arms around her Trista pushed him away.

She finally came to her senses. "What the hell, Blake? How long has this been going on?"

"This was the first time. I swear, Trista. Cherie came over to show the condo, and the customer cancelled at the last minute." Blake ran a hand through his wet, sandy-blond hair. "One thing led to another...Hell, I don't know. It just happened."

"You want me to believe this has only happened once?" Trista asked, incredulous. It was like the fog had been lifted from her mind. She *knew* in her heart this wasn't his first time. How could she be so blind for so long? She didn't even wait for him to give an answer. "Get out!"

"What? Trista, this is nothing. I swear. I love you, babe."

"Get out!" she repeated, pointing to the sliding glass doors. "NOW! I don't want to ever see you again."

"Trista, let's talk about this. You just got fired. You need me. You can't..."

"Wait a minute. I never said I got fired. I only said the meeting didn't go well. How did you know?"

Blake surprised her by laughing.

"What's so fucking funny?" she asked, the sick feeling in her stomach growing larger by the second.

"I knew about this."

"What are you talking about?" Trista looked confused.

"Gil called me last night and told me they weren't going to renew your contract."

Trista clenched her teeth. She felt hot all over as her blood pressure shot up. Her face felt like it was on fire. "You knew I was getting fired and you didn't tell me?"

"Gil asked me not too." Blake threw the towel down and walked inside, leaving a trail of wet footprints on the Brazilian cherry hardwood floor. Trista followed him as he started to put on his clothes. "Face it, Trista. You've gotten stale. The viewers have noticed, the producers have noticed—hell, your whole crew knows it. The only person who hasn't noticed is you. You think you're the only reason why the show is doing so good?" Hastily, he tucked in his striped Oxford shirt and slipped on his shoes, not bothering to wait for her response. "The thing is you're the one who is bringing the show down. Gil wanted to let you go last season, but *I* convinced him to give you another season. You should be fucking thanking *me*."

Trista sank down on the bed. She couldn't believe what she was hearing. Not only had Blake cheated on her, but he had betrayed her as well. She had endured enough for one day. Standing up, she smacked him across the face, leaving an angry, red imprint on his cheek. "You're an asshole. WE. ARE. DONE. Get the fuck out and don't bother coming back. I'll send your things to the office!"

He rubbed his cheek. "You'll regret this." Blake picked up his wallet and keys from the nightstand and walked to the door. "You can't make it in this town without me. You'll be blackballed from every production company in Hollywood!"

Trista fell to the floor and burst into tears as the front door slammed.

Chapter Three

Trista Carmichael smiled when she passed over the Florida state line. She was only a couple hours away from her destination. It had been a long, three-day drive from California, and she was looking forward to spending time at the beach. Sugar-white sands, turquoise blue waters, and brilliant sunshine were just what the doctor ordered.

She still couldn't believe after spending three years on a hit TV show and winning two Golden Globe awards for "best television actress," not to mention her latest SAG award, she was suddenly without a job. And without a fiancé, with whom she had wasted two years of her life. Who knew how many other sluts he had bonked while she was working her ass off? Trista's love life and her career were simultaneously over in a matter of hours. The only good thing that came out of Blake's fling with the Realtor was a full-price cash offer on her condo. As soon as escrow had closed on her place, she was out the door. Out of Hollywood. Goodbye California! The only place she could think to go that was far from California and her previous life was to Florida, where the beach could soothe her broken heart and heal her wounded soul.

After a grueling drive, Trista was almost home—although the thought of facing her older sister, Nicolette, made her want to turn around and drive back. In order to face her estranged sister, Trista needed a stiff drink. Or two. Or three. They hadn't spoken in two years, and Nicolette had no idea Trista was coming home. Even though she had spent the last few years getting her acting career off the ground, first in New York, then California, Trista still considered Florida her home. It's where she grew up. Her family still lived here.

The Liar's Club was a well-known local bar, and it was down the street from Trista's beach house. She pulled her convertible into the parking lot of the rundown bar. Only two trucks graced the lot. She took a moment to stretch her legs when she got out of the car, groaning at the stiffness. It was almost eleven o'clock in the evening, and the Liar's Club would be closing soon, but she still had time to throw down a couple of drinks.

The Liar's Club was detached from the seafood restaurant next to it. It had a large L-shaped counter with around twenty barstools. Patrons from the restaurant next door would come in for drinks while they waited for their tables to come available. During the fall, locals would flock to the bar to watch football games on the big screen TV's, which were mounted throughout the lounge area and bar. The Liar's Club also served typical bar food like chicken wings, sliders, raw oysters, and nachos. However, tonight, Trista wanted a drink. Or two.

"What'll ya have?" the bartender asked as soon as she sat down on the barstool. There was only one other customer, and he was passed out cold at the other end of the bar.

"Certainly not whatever you gave him," she answered, nodding toward the only other guest.

The bartender laughed. "Don't mind Crazy Jack. He had a rough day. His dog died. Wife left him. And he lost his job."

"Sounds like the beginnings of a bad country song."

"Exactly."

Trista flashed a smile at the handsome bartender. "I'll take a margarita. On the rocks. No salt."

"Never seen you around here," he said, making small talk.

"Is that your best pickup line?"

"Stick around. The more you drink, the better they get." He plucked a bottle of tequila from the glass shelf. "However, it is the middle of February. The only people, who are in town now, besides the locals, are snowbirds. And you're not quite old enough to qualify as a snowbird."

"I'm hoping it's a compliment," Trista said. She knew he was referring to snowbirds as an affectionate term for the elderly winter guests who frequented the Florida beaches during the off-season. "I'm visiting family, if you must know."

He set her drink down in front of her, a hint of a smile on his face. "My name's Riker. Let me know if you need something else."

Trista watched as he turned around to change the TV channel. His jeans were tight in all the right places, the black t-shirt accentuated his muscular arms, and his dark hair hung a few inches below his collar. The deep tan suggested he probably spent his free days on the water. Surfing most likely. His crystal-blue eyes matched the color of the Gulf of Mexico on a calm day. The three-day stubble on his face and deep dimples when he smiled made Trista think naughty thoughts.

She took a sip of her drink. It was one of the best margaritas she had ever tasted. The first hit of the drink was tangy followed by a sweet, smooth finish. Trista considered herself a connoisseur of the margarita; it was her go-to drink of choice. Most of her girlfriends were wine or champagne lovers. Not her. She loved the taste of good tequila mixed with lime juice. Trista hated the ones that left a sour, bitter aftertaste in her mouth, which was usually because the bartender had used a cheap mix and low-grade tequila. She preferred top-shelf brands, like Silver Patron or Casa Dragones. "This is a damn good margarita."

"Thank you," Riker said, putting limes in a Tupperware bowl. "Margaritas are one of my specialties. The key is to use lots of real limes…and a secret ingredient."

She wondered what else he specialized in. "Which is?" she asked, referring to the special ingredient.

"I don't give away my secrets to pretty women I just met."

"I'm sure I can get it out of you," Trista said, her boldness surprising herself. She was being very flirty with him, which was unlike her. She never made the first move, or flirted with strangers. What exactly did he put in this drink? She drank three more trying to figure it out. All the while watching Riker work the bar. Wiping down counters, putting away the limes, drying glasses, and sweeping the floor. There was something intoxicating about the way he moved around the bar. Or maybe she had too much to drink. And was horny as hell. She hadn't been with anyone since Blake. And that was over a month ago.

"It's almost closing time. If you stick around for a few minutes, I'll walk you to your car."

"I'm a big girl. I think I can make it home in this very rough area of town," Trista said sarcastically, hopping off her barstool and then immediately regretting it. The whole room seemed to tilt. She quickly grabbed the side of the bar top.

Riker watched her stumble. He picked up his cell phone. "Let me call a cab for Crazy Jack, and then we'll get out of this place. I can drive you home."

Trista regained her balance and made it to the bathroom while Riker closed down the bar. The restrooms were at the back of the bar near the pool tables and dartboards. Along the back wall, the owners of the bar had put up pictures of celebrities who had frequented the bar. There were quite a few country singers, TV and movie stars, and politicians who came to Blue Mountain Beach. A few even had second homes here. The pristine beaches and crystal waters were comparable to the Caribbean, but cheaper and more conveniently located. Trista noticed her picture was still up on the wall. Her hair was darker and wavy, and she was about twenty pounds heavier and ten years younger. The photo had been taken at the beginning of her career. She looked like a totally different person now. She wondered if Riker knew who she was. If he did, he didn't let on. Trista quickly used the facilities and washed up, splashing cold water on her face. Those margaritas had done a number on her. Thank goodness her beach house was only a couple miles down the road.

"Ready to go?" Riker called from the bar as she exited the restroom.

"Coming." Trista desperately hoped her sister was asleep when she got home. Even after three strong drinks, she wasn't ready to face Nicolette. All she wanted to do was take a hot bath and go to bed.

Outside, the air was cool and breezy. The smell of briny salt air was comforting to Trista. She felt she'd made the right decision in coming home.

"Well, it was nice to meet you." Riker watched as she got in her car. "You know, I never got your name."

"You never asked," Trista said closing her door. The top was still down on her Mercedes. She pulled a baseball cap off the dashboard and put it on.

"Are you sure you're okay to drive?" Riker leaned over and rested his forearms on her door. "At least let me follow you home."

"I'm a little down the road. I'll be okay."

"If you insist." She watched as Riker got in his truck. He tried to turn over the engine, but the truck wouldn't cooperate. He banged his hand on the steering wheel in frustration. Trista continued to watch as he got out of the truck and opened the hood. After tinkering around for minute, he slammed it shut. He walked back to her car.

"How about a ride home?"

"Get in," she laughed. "Where am I taking you?"

"I'm across the highway off Sugar Drive. You know how to get there?"

"Yeah, I do." Trista pushed a button and watched as the convertible top eased back in place. She carefully backed the Mercedes out of the lot and headed away from the beach.

Five minutes later, she pulled up to a large subdivision situated on a lake and surrounded by Point Washington State Forest. The subdivision had several townhome units as well as single-family dwellings. Riker lived in one of the townhomes. Trista knew the development very well. Her father had originally been one of the developers on the project, but she didn't mention it to Riker.

"Would you like to come in for a drink? It's the least I can do for the ride home." Riker smiled, his dimples popping up.

Trista leaned over the seat and brushed her lips against Riker's. She breathed in his scent. Leather, woodsy, smoke, with a hint of something else. Vanilla? It was heavenly.

"I've been wanting to do that since you walked into the bar," Riker said before kissing her back. He slipped his tongue into her mouth and placed his hand on the back of her neck. She loved the way he tasted.

And the way he kissed, slow and gentle. "How about we take this inside where it's more comfortable?" Riker suggested after a few minutes had passed.

Trista got out of the car and followed him inside. His home was surprisingly clean and organized. Her ex-fiancé, Blake, was never clean—he was actually a pig in more than one sense of the word. Constantly leaving his underwear and socks all over the condo. Newspapers and magazines strewn about the place. Trista had employed a full-time housekeeper to keep up with Blake's mess. She was glad she didn't have to put up with it anymore.

"Have a seat," Riker said, leading her to a black leather couch. "I'll make us a drink."

Trista sank down into the soft, buttery leather. She observed Riker as he made his way into the kitchen. The living room, dining area, and kitchen were all situated in one large room, open and airy. The walls were adorned with framed posters of past seafood festivals and fishing rodeos. A large blue marlin hung above the fireplace. It was apparent what Riker's favorite pastimes were.

As she studied the various artworks, Riker walked back with two drinks in his hands. He handed one to her.

"What's this?"

"Something light." Riker took a sip of his drink. "Try it," he said as Trista stared into her drink. Taking a sip, she was pleasantly surprised by the bubbles tickling her tongue. The drink was crisp and cool. "Prosecco?"

"Right." He flashed a grin at her. "With a splash of peach puree."

"It's delicious." Trista took another sip.

"You know, before we go any further, I think you should tell me your name. I mean it's only fair. I told you mine."

"Trista Carmichael." She waited for his reaction. Surely he'd guessed by now who she was. But he only nodded, sticking out his hand. She placed her glass on the coffee table before taking his hand.

"Nice to meet you, Miss Carmichael."

She tightened her grip and pulled him closer to her. "Let's forget the small talk." *What the fuck am I doing?* The sensible side of her was thinking…she was sitting in a stranger's apartment, drinking some fruity drink, and thinking about having sex. The naughty side of her was thinking…God, I'm so fucking horny. Here's a handsome guy who makes one hell of a margarita and lives in a decent home plus he apparently has no idea who I am. *Go for it.* The naughty side won out.

She kissed him again. Her tongue exploring his mouth. Their kiss was warm and passionate, and it drove her crazy with desire. Trista had never felt like this with Blake…or hell, anyone else for that matter. She wanted Riker's lips to explore every part of her body. His hand reached up her blouse and caressed her breasts through her bra. She moaned when he lifted the bra and slipped his fingers inside, caressing a nipple. They continued to kiss while he played with each breast, gently rubbing and teasing each one.

"Hang on a second," Trista said, pulling back. She stood up and took off her shirt and bra. And in one smooth movement, pulled off her jeans. She smiled as Riker studied her. He reached out and pulled her onto his lap. He nestled his head on her neck and kissed her before making his way down to her nipple, sucking and flicking with his tongue. Trista moaned as he continued to take the nipple in his mouth, tugging gently then scraping his teeth across it. He had one hand on her back and slipped the other inside of her panties. She could feel his manhood hard, ready to go. He used his finger to explore her, rubbing her clit with his thumb.

"Oh my God, you're so wet. You feel so good," Riker said, as Trista tilted her head back and let out a sigh. He was quickly bringing her to an orgasm. She came so hard and so fast, she almost blacked out from the intensity of it. He wasted no time, scooping her up and carrying her to his bedroom.

Trista was so relaxed, her body felt like rubber, as Riker laid her down on silky cool sheets. She watched as he peeled off his t-shirt then his jeans and underwear. He was like a Roman god standing before her with hard muscles rippling throughout his tanned body. His thick cock was large and impressive. He reached over and pulled open the drawer on the nightstand, grasping a foil wrapper. Unwrapping the condom, he rolled it on expertly with one hand before climbing on top of Trista. She could feel his erection pressing against her thigh. "I can't wait any longer. Please," Trista said.

"Please what?" Riker teased, running his hands through her hair, kissing her neck.

"Put your cock inside of me."

"I'm going to take it nice and slow," he said, sliding into her with one long stroke, "before making you come, again and again." Trista felt herself melt into the silky sheets as he eased in and out of her. Her pussy stretching to accommodate every inch of him, filling her up completely. It may have been the delicious drinks Riker made her or the fact she hadn't had proper sex in many months. Whatever it was, she knew she would be seeing a lot of Riker.

Chapter Four

Early the next morning, Trista slipped out of Riker's bed while he was still sleeping. Her beach house was a short drive away in Blue Mountain Beach. Trista had bought the house as an investment when she made her first few million dollars in Hollywood. At the time, she was still speaking with her sister, Nicolette. Trista invited Nicolette to live in the home and watch over things while Trista was working in Hollywood. In the beginning, Trista would fly back to Florida during the holidays and see her family. After she had a major falling out with Nicolette, Trista didn't come home anymore. Hurt feelings and words that couldn't be taken back still haunted Trista.

Driving down Old Blue Mountain Beach Road, Trista smiled at the sight of the magnificent beachfront estates lining the gulf-front road. She had picked this part of the beach due to its privacy and exclusivity. It was also within walking distance to many of her favorite places. For the Health of It was her favorite juice bar and health food store, and there was Marie's Bistro, where she could get a delicious sushi dinner, and Sally's By The Sea, which was a gas station, deli, and sundries shop all rolled into one. Plus Sally's had the best hamburgers on the beach.

Pulling up to her gated estate, she entered a code for the electronic gate to open. Her three-story beach villa never failed to take her breath away. It was luxurious and opulent—all three stories with stunning Gulf views from every angle. The villa had six bedrooms and eight baths, ten balconies, a lanai porch, saltwater pool with Jacuzzi, stone exterior entry, and a three-car garage, all under an 8,095-square-foot roof. The first floor showcased a balustrade parlor, media room, and wet bar in addition to two guest rooms with spa baths. A grand, circular staircase led to the second floor also with sweeping Gulf views and a great room with gourmet kitchen and dining room, which was perfect for entertaining. Her sister had one of the large bedrooms and spa bath on this level. The third floor was Trista's favorite. It included a fitness studio, health bar, and makeup studio. Her master bedroom suite had a luxury spa bath and panoramic views of the Gulf.

Trista felt mixed emotions as she pulled into the driveway and opened the garage door. She loved being at the beach, but she dreaded the thought of having to deal with her sister. She breathed a sigh of relief when she realized no one was home. The garage was empty as Trista parked her convertible inside. She pulled her overnight bag out of the trunk and headed inside.

First things first. Trista took the stairs to the second level and threw her bag down on the breakfast table in the kitchen area. She popped a K-cup in the Keurig and started a cup of coffee. Taking a look around, she realized not much had changed. The house was still as she'd left it two years ago.

Trista picked up her coffee cup and checked the refrigerator for creamer. Finding a stocked fridge, Trista added a splash of French Vanilla creamer to her coffee. She took her cup and wandered to the lanai. There was a comfy couch covered in off-white denim fabric, four matching chairs, and a chaise lounge artfully arranged on the patio. A coffee table held a large, crystal bowl stuffed with sand dollars and seashells. Trista plopped down on one of the chairs and rested her feet on the ottoman. She breathed in the fresh, salty air. With a steaming hot cup of coffee by her side, she watched the waves slowly rolling in as seagulls dove in and out of the Gulf of Mexico, searching for their breakfast. She spotted a pod of dolphins a few feet offshore, playing in the water. Their water acrobatics never failed to thrill her. She continued to watch as the dolphins jumped and flipped down the coast. God, she didn't realize how much she'd missed the beach. Yeah, California had beaches but nothing compared to the beaches of the Emerald Coast.

She was lost in her thoughts of the mind-blowing sex with Riker and didn't hear the French doors open.

"What the hell are you doing here?"

Trista turned to see her sister standing behind her. Nicolette was wearing a colorful, paisley beach cover-up, flip-flops, and a baseball cap that covered her long, dark hair. Where Trista was blonde, tall, and slim, Nicolette was shorter and struggled with her weight. Trista had inherited her mother's beautiful looks, while Nicolette looked a lot like their father. Trista knew her sister was pretty, but her attitude made her ugly sometimes.

"This is my house. In case you forgot." Trista couldn't help the bite of sarcasm in her voice.

"Why are you here?" Nicolette pulled off her cap and shook her wet hair off her shoulders.

"It's a long story. Why don't you have a seat?" Trista picked up her mug and took a sip of her coffee. She decided to get right to the point. "I got fired from my job."

Nicolette's face softened as she sighed. She sat across from Trista on the chaise lounge. "What happened?"

"They told me the show needed to go in another direction."

"Sorry 'bout that. But you can get another one, right?"

Trista shrugged then added, "Blake was cheating on me. It's over."

Nicolette looked confused. "Wait a minute. Who's Blake?"

Trista laughed despite the uneasiness between them. "I guess it's been a long while since we talked. Blake and I were engaged."

"Blake is your agent, right?"

"*Was* my agent. I fired him, but not before I kicked him out. I sold the condo, packed my stuff, and headed here. I got in last night." Trista drained the rest of her coffee. "Where were you this morning?"

"I spent the night with a girlfriend. We had a girl's night out, and I crashed at her place." Nicolette stood and picked up her things. "How long are you planning on staying?"

"Not sure yet. Is that a problem?"

"I guess not. It is *your* place." Nicolette checked her watch. "Shit, I'm running late. I've got a sales meeting in fifteen minutes and a busy day ahead." Nicolette waited a beat. "I'm throwing a surprise birthday party for my boyfriend, James, tonight. Here at the house."

"Don't worry about me, Nic. I'm planning on relaxing today and going to bed early. I won't get in your way."

Nicolette paused at the door. "Party starts at seven. Dress is casual. You can come if you want."

"Are you sure?"

She nodded.

"Okay. I'll see you then." Trista watched as her sister left the room. It was like nothing had happened between them. Nicolette was just like their father in that way. If there was a problem, sweep it under the rug.

Forget about it. Trista liked to talk things out. If she was going to stay here for a while then she needed to clear the air with her sister. But they would do it later—after the party. She hated to ruin a good party.

Chapter Five

Trista waltzed into the Beach Peach Boutique—one of her favorite places to shop in Blue Mountain Beach. They carried all her preferred clothing brands. She loved the smell of coconut, lime, and verbena candles the store kept lit throughout the day. A woman with an armful of clothes approached her. "Hey, I know you. From the show, *You Only Live Once*? Right? Trista Carmichael?"

Trista was used to people recognizing her on the streets of LA. Most of them never approached her though. Sometimes they took discreet photos from a distance. However, whenever she visited small towns, people were friendly and approached her with requests of autographs or photos with their cell phones.

Trista pulled a chiffon coral maxi-dress with spaghetti straps from the rack. "Yep, that's me."

"I can't believe the network fired you," the woman said, thrusting her bundle of clothes at the salesgirl who approached them. "Are you going to work on another show?"

As soon as the news broke about her dismissal from the show, and about the embarrassing breakup with Blake, her face was plastered on all the Hollywood rags, like *OK! Magazine*, *People*, and *STAR*. Trista flashed a friendly smile at the woman. “No, I’m taking a well-needed vacation right now.”

“Can I have a picture with you?” The woman pulled out her cell phone. She was wearing a brightly colored beach cover-up, flip-flops, and a sun visor placed on top of her frizzy red hair. Typical Florida tourist beach wear. Trista guessed the fan was in her late forties. “My friends aren’t going to believe I ran into you! We’re here on vacation too. I never thought I would see my favorite TV star!” The woman continued to gush while Trista stood next to her and the salesgirl took a quick picture. “Thank you so much!”

“You’re quite welcome.”

“Listen, hon, I wouldn’t worry about what the press is saying about you. And the fiancé you had? He’s a bad, bad boy. I can tell by looking at his picture in the magazine.” The woman reached in her bag and pulled out the latest copy of *In Touch* magazine, showing it to her. Trista was surprised to see her and Blake on the cover. She tried to stay away from reading half-truths in these so-called Hollywood rags. The title screamed, “**TRISTA CARMICHAEL & BLAKE SIMMONS CALL OFF WEDDING?**” There was an insert of a smaller picture of Blake with another gorgeous, blonde woman on his arm. Trista recognized her as Melanie Sweetwater. She was another actress rumored to have slept around with more producers and directors than any other wannabe actress in the history of Hollywood. “You are much prettier than she is.”

Trista wasn’t sure how to respond to the comment. Instead she put a smile on her face and thanked the lady for her support, handing the dress to the salesgirl after the fan-girl moment. “Can I try this on?”

"Of course. I'll start a dressing room for you." The salesgirl pulled a white crocheted cardigan from a mannequin. "This looks great with the maxi. You know, for the cooler weather we're having now."

"Thank you." Trista liked the way the cardigan was made with lightweight material, perfect for the beach. "I'll try it too." She wanted to look nice for the party tonight. If she was going to work things out with Nicolette, then she needed to get to know her sister's friends and boyfriend. Trista was going to make it her top priority while she was here in Florida. And finding a new job. She slipped into the dressing room and tried on the clothes.

"I'm sorry about that," the salesgirl said discreetly when Trista walked out of the dressing room. "Most people in this town mind their own business."

"It's okay," Trista answered. She twirled around, viewing herself in the full-length mirror. The coral dress fit her perfectly. "I'm used to it."

"I heard you had a beach house here in Blue Mountain. Of course, no one has ever seen you around, so I thought it was a rumor," the salesgirl continued.

"I'm visiting family," Trista answered. She wandered around the store and picked out two more dresses. One was an off-shoulder sundress in mint, and another maxi dress, this one peach, with a white crochet insert at the hem and neckline. Spring was right around the corner, and she needed a few new things to spice up her wardrobe. Most of her things she left behind in California in an air-conditioned storage unit. Starting over seemed like a good idea when she left.

"Do you have a big event to attend?"

"A private birthday party." Trista added a few pieces of jewelry and a pair of bone-colored sandals to the mix. "I'll try these on, too. Thanks."

Trista slipped back into the dressing room and tried on the rest of the clothes. After her breakup with Blake, Trista had lost a few pounds. A few years ago, she would've been happy with the sudden weight loss. When she first moved to Hollywood her agent at the time—a gentleman named Walter Murphy, who had since retired—advised her to lose about twenty pounds if she wanted to work in the film business. Trista struggled for months to lose the weight, spending money she didn't have on personal trainers and protein-shake mixes. Now a five-pound weight loss made her look too thin. She vowed to eat right while she was here. Florida was known for its fresh seafood, and she planned to indulge herself in shrimp, scallops, fish, and lobster, along with decadent key lime pies. Trista walked out of the dressing room in the mint sundress, admiring the way the dress hugged her frame. The spray tan she'd gotten before she came to Florida really accentuated the color.

"The dress looks really good on you!" the salesgirl told her. "It brings out your complexion nicely."

Trista studied herself in the mirror again. The mint dress hugged her curves in all the right places. Her trademark honey-blonde hair hung loosely around her shoulders. She had inherited her mother's unusual violet-blue eyes, pert nose, and full lips. Her father, who was Italian, thankfully passed on his nice skin color to her. She thought she got the best of both worlds from her parents. She turned full circle and admired the way the dress looked on her. "I'll take everything," she told the salesgirl. She headed back to the dressing room and changed.

She was a little nervous about the party tonight. She wondered if Nicolette had told her friends about her famous sister. "Is the Watercolor Spa still open?" Trista inquired as she put all the clothing and shoes on the sales counter. What she really needed was a full day of pampering. Massage, facial, mani-pedi…and thinking about her wild night with Riker, a bikini wax. Who knows? After the party, Trista thought, she might head over to the Liar's Club and see if Riker was working. Another night of hot, passionate sex could be the cure she needed for a broken heart.

"Yes, it is. My friend Ella works there. I can call her and set something up for you. She'll take good care of you," she offered as she rang up the purchases.

Trista looked at her watch. It was almost noon. "That would be great. I need to run if I'm going to make the party in time." She thanked the salesgirl, grabbed her bags, and headed out to the spa. Tonight she wasn't going to worry about Blake or her career. She would focus on having fun with her sister and making new friends.

Chapter Six

Trista could hear the guests arriving as she dressed. She was surprised to find she had butterflies in her stomach. Attending this party would be a start in the right direction with her sister. Plus she was curious about meeting Nicolette's new boyfriend. She had never known Nicolette to be in a serious relationship with anyone. Normally she went from one man to the next, getting out before the relationship turned serious. Trista thought her sister secretly sabotaged her own relationships so she wouldn't get hurt. She imagined it had something to do with her own parent's fucked-up relationship.

Trista's bedroom had a panoramic view of the Gulf of Mexico with floor-to-ceiling windows. A custom-made, king-size, round bed took up the middle of the room. Trista's decorator spared no expense when it came to decorating her house, especially the master suite. Everything was made specially for this room, including bedding worth thousands of dollars: silk comforters and throw pillows, five-thousand-thread-count sheets of Egyptian cotton, all done in soft hues of lavender, grey, and yellow. Handmade furniture and local artwork by Carl Coleman adorned the walls. She wondered why Nicolette had never moved into the master bedroom after her long absence. Trista had been gone for two years, with only the occasional visit. Yet her sister stayed in one of the guest rooms on the second floor.

She glanced in the mirror and applied her favorite Urban Decay lip gloss. She had the hairdresser at the spa do a blowout on her honey-blonde hair, making it shiny and smooth. The facial and body scrub she received made her complexion glow from head to toe. Her toenails had been applied with OPI Cajun Shrimp, to complement the coral maxi was she wearing, and her fingernails had a couple coats of Essie Tennis Corset, a white polish with a touch of glitter. She felt more like herself than she had since her split with Blake. Trista didn't know if it was the day at the spa and new clothes or the great sex. Either way, she planned on more of all of it in the coming weeks—her self-prescribed medicine.

Trista took a deep breath. "It's now or never," she said before heading out. Once downstairs she found around fifty people gathered in the open living room. Nicolette had hired a party planner to help with the event. The whole place was decorated festively with silver and white balloons, glittering candles, and fresh white roses. Everyone stopped in mid-conversation and stared at Trista as she entered the room. Nicolette looked up from her conversation with a group of girls, her eyes on Trista as she walked toward her. Nicolette cleared her throat. "Um, everyone. We have a special guest tonight. This is Trista Carmichael. My sister."

Trista blushed uncomfortably. She registered the shocked look on the guests' faces and heard the murmuring of the crowd. So Nicolette hadn't told her friends about her. It was typical. Her sister didn't want Trista to steal her spotlight.

"I didn't know Trista Carmichael was Nicolette's sister?"

"What? How is that possible? I thought she was an only child!"

"Didn't she get fired from that show?"

"Hello, everyone! I look forward to meeting all of you personally. First, I need a drink!" Trista gave an awkward laugh before heading into the kitchen. The caterers were setting up a large buffet with fresh Florida seafood, corn on the cob, cheese grits, and a variety of desserts. Trista grabbed a champagne flute from a silver tray sitting on the kitchen counter. She took a hearty gulp, trying to steady her nerves.

"You handled it well," Nicolette said from behind her.

"You never told anyone we were sisters? Are you ashamed of me?"

"No, it never came up."

"Will we ever be able to put our differences behind us?" Trista asked.

"This is not the time to discuss *our differences*. James will be here any minute now, and this is supposed to be his surprise party. The key word being *surprise*."

"Okay Nicolette. But we can't kept putting this off forever."

"He's coming!" One of the girls shouted from the living room. "Everyone hide!"

"Tomorrow then," Nicolette said, grabbing her sister's hand. "Tonight we have fun! Come on."

Nicolette hit the lights, darkening the living room. Only a few candles glittered throughout the area. "He thinks we're having a romantic dinner. Just the two of us. I had everyone park their cars down the road at the neighbor's house. Wait until he sees all of his friends here. He'll be knocked out of his socks," she whispered to Trista, still holding on to her hand. For a moment, it felt like they were still little girls playing hide and seek in their bedroom.

Everyone got quiet as the front door opened. Trista could make out a tall figure standing in the doorway. "Nicolette?" he called out. "Where are you?"

Trista sucked in a breath. Suddenly the lights came on, silver and white balloons and colorful confetti dropped from the high ceiling, and everyone shouted, "SURPRISE!"

Standing in the doorway was Nicolette's boyfriend. He was the epitome of tall, dark, and handsome, wearing distressed jeans and a white, button-down shirt. Canvas deck shoes on his feet. He genuinely looked surprised as his eyes met Nicolette's. Then he saw Trista.

"Shit, shit, shit," Trista mumbled under her breath as her eyes locked with Riker, Nicolette's boyfriend. James and Riker were one and the same. She dropped Nicolette's hand like a hot potato. "He's knocked out of his socks, all right," Trista whispered.

Chapter Seven

"Trista, I want you to meet my boyfriend, James Riker." Nicolette held his hand tightly. "James, this is my sister, Trista Carmichael."

He shook her hand with a bewildered smile on face. "Nice to meet you, Trista." Riker turned his attention to Nicolette. "You never told me you had a sister."

"Well, Trista has been in Hollywood the last couple of years. She's here for a *quick* visit."

Trista noticed her sister put an emphasis on the word quick. After Nicolette finds out I slept with her boyfriend, I won't be able to get out of here fast enough, she thought.

"Hollywood, huh? What do you do there?" Riker asked, an amused look on his handsome face.

Trista could see he was struggling to maintain the conversation. All she wanted to do was go back upstairs and hide under the covers. She had slept with her sister's boyfriend. How in the hell were they going to fix their relationship now? Nicolette would never forgive her. And why was Riker cheating on Nicolette? It was one thing she wouldn't tolerate—once a cheater, always a cheater. That was why she and Blake would never work out. Trista had been through enough cheating scandals in her life. She thought about her father and how his cheating had caused the original rift between her and Nicolette.

"She was on the show, *You Only Live Once*," Nicolette said.

"So, you're an actress?" he asked her, genuinely surprise.

Trista nodded as Riker studied her with renewed interest.

"I forgot. The only TV James watches is the sports channel. I don't think he has ever seen anything else on TV other than a football game.

"*The Simpsons*," Riker said.

"Huh?" Nicolette asked.

"I watch *The Simpsons* on Sunday nights."

"Right. Anyway, let's go get you a beer." Nicolette led Riker away while Trista stood in shock. She didn't know what was worse. Her sister dating a cheater or her sister finding out that Trista was the one who'd slept with her boyfriend.

For the rest of the party Trista managed to avoid Riker. She would leave a room when she saw him enter and find somewhere else to hang out. After a couple of hours, though, she got tired of the cat-and-mouse game. Trista went upstairs and changed into a pair of sweatpants and a t-shirt. Quietly, she slipped out the back door and headed for the soft, sandy beach. If not for the surprise party, this would have been a perfect night. The moon was full, the waves were softly crashing onto the beach, and the air was cool but not too cold. Trista relished the feeling of the powdery sand between her toes as she made her way down to the water.

Dipping her foot into the chilly salt water, she thought about how all this was going to play out. She already had a hard road ahead of her if she was going to repair her relationship with Nicolette. Now she was going to have to come clean about sleeping with Riker. Nicolette deserved to know Riker was sleeping around on her. Trista hadn't known Riker had a girlfriend, let alone, that girlfriend being her sister. Nicolette would have to forgive her. Trista couldn't have known Riker was her boyfriend. Hell, he had introduced himself as Riker. Everyone at the party called him Riker, she noticed. But her sister was the only one who called him by his first name, James. Nicolette would understand the situation. It was a mistake. A mistake Trista would not let happen again.

Trista continued to walk farther down the beach, away from the house with all the noise and drunken partygoers. She sat down at the base of a sand dune and contemplated going back to Hollywood. Or maybe she should go to New York. Her career had started on Broadway with a bit part. Plus, she'd done a short stint on a daytime soap opera. There were plenty of possibilities. She would call her new agent, Kate Peterson, tomorrow morning and let her know to put out some feelers on any new gigs opening up. Trista had started her career with Kate, so it was only fitting Kate find her a new job. Start over fresh somewhere. Trista started to get excited about the prospect of moving to New York. She would buy a condo in trendy Tribeca. Eat leisurely brunches at Popovers on Amsterdam and 86th Street. Take long walks in Central Park. See a Yankees game. All her favorite things to do in the Big Apple.

"Hey, Trista. I've been looking all over for you." A male voice interrupted her thoughts. "Can we talk for a minute?"

Trista looked up to see Riker standing at the foot of the dune. "You're the last person I want to talk to." Trista waved him away. "Leave me alone please."

"I want a chance to explain."

Trista scoffed. "Save it for Nicolette. You owe her an explanation, not me."

"It's over between me and Nicolette." Riker walked closer to Trista. So close she could smell his delicious scent. He irritated her and intrigued her all at once.

"Of course it is…now. Or it will be once she knows about you." Trista brushed the sand off her pants as she stood up. "How long have you been running around on her?"

"You don't understand. It's *been* over between Nicolette and me. We aren't together anymore."

"She introduced you as her boyfriend." Trista pushed Riker as hard as she could. Caught off guard, he stumbled and fell back on his rear end. "I don't know what kind of bullshit you're trying to pull, but you aren't going to hurt my sister."

"I don't want to hurt Nicolette." Riker reached up and pulled on Trista's ankle, which caused her to fall on top of him. He wrapped his arms around her, holding on to her tightly. "Obviously you guys had a little falling out. She didn't even tell me about you."

"That has nothing to do with you. Don't change the subject. You've been sleeping around on her. Exactly how many women have you been with?" Trista tried to wiggle out of his strong grasp.

"I haven't been sleeping around. First of all, we aren't dating anymore. Second, when we were dating, I never cheated on her. Regardless of what you think, I don't go around fucking everything that moves. And if I remember correctly, you were a willing participant last night."

"I didn't know my sister was in love with you!" Trista felt comforted, and irritated at the same time with Riker's arms tightly around her.

"Please listen to me. Nicolette and I broke up months ago. She's not fond of the word *no*. I've told her several times we were never going to be a couple again. Lately, it's only been a casual thing between us. A few nights ago, we had dinner. She asked me to give her one more chance. I told her we would see how it goes, but I made it clear we were not exclusive. This party," Riker paused, pointing to the beach house in the distance, "was a complete surprise to me. I had no idea." He put his hand on top of hers and held it over his chest. "I'm telling you the truth."

Trista wasn't sure about anything he was saying. He was right about one thing. Her sister wasn't fond of the word *no*. Nicolette always wanted the things she couldn't have and would do anything to get what she wanted. But all that didn't matter. Nicolette was her sister. Despite everything that had happened between them, Trista didn't want to hurt her. Whether or not Riker was telling the truth didn't matter. Obviously, Nicolette still had feelings for him.

However, Trista was having a hard time resisting this man. She tried to block out the strong emotions she was feeling for Riker right now. The way he smelled delicious, his strong arms that were wrapped around her, the memories of their night of passionate sex. There was something about Riker she couldn't deny. It was like he had some kind of spell on her, and she didn't think she could help herself if she stayed another second.

"I need to go." Trista tried to stand up, but Riker pulled her back down. He put his hands on her face and pulled her closer before kissing her. She felt herself go limp in his arms. She couldn't help it. She kissed him back. "I can't do this," she said between kisses.

"Yes, you can. I know you feel it too." Riker kissed her again. "You and I were made for each other, Trista Carmichael."

"I don't want to hurt my sister."

"Whatever problems you and Nicolette have...don't have anything to do with

us. I want you," Riker whispered, slipping his hand up her shirt. He caressed her right nipple sending a fluttering sensation to her stomach. Before she knew it, her sweatpants were down around her ankles and Riker was on top of her. She could feel his erection stretching the fabric of his jeans. "I need to get inside of you."

Trista couldn't resist him. She wanted this man unlike any other she had been with before. She reached down and unzipped his jeans. Riker pulled his pants down and she freed his cock from his underwear. Trista put her hand around it and stroked the length of it, causing Riker to moan in her ear.

"You turn me on so bad," he said, clenching his jaw. He slipped a finger inside of her, feeling her wetness. "I love feeling how wet you get for me."

"I want to feel you inside me, right now," Trista said, pulling him down on top of her.

She sucked in a deep breath when he slipped inside of her, filling every inch of her with his beautiful cock. This is the last time, she told herself. After tonight, she was going to work things out with her sister, for better or for worse.

Chapter Eight

After saying goodbye to Riker, Trista walked back to the party, stopping by the deck to rinse the sand off her feet. She managed to avoid her sister and all the guests by using the garage entrance and taking the elevator up to her room on the third floor. She stripped off her clothes and stepped inside a hot shower.

A gamut of emotions ran through her. Part of her was disgusted with herself for having sex with Riker again. Especially after knowing Nicolette was head over heels in love with the man. Riker told her repeatedly it was over with him and Nicolette. But it shouldn't matter, Trista thought. Nicolette would still be hurt if she knew Riker was having sex with her younger sister.

But the other part of her felt an undeniable attraction to Riker. Conflicting emotions were making her crazy. She had no choice now but to leave town. First thing tomorrow, she was going to call her agent and start planning to move to New York. She would have the movers ship her boxes out of storage in California and send them to New York. Far away from Riker, her sister, and Blue Mountain Beach.

The next morning Trista awoke to the smell of bacon, eggs, and coffee. She felt a little stiff and sore, remembering her rendezvous with Riker at the beach last night. Trista felt a confusing sense of remorse and happiness. She tried to think it through. Riker was someone she'd recently met. Why did she feel such a pull to this man? It was purely sexual attraction, she reasoned. She didn't know one thing about him except he had dated her sister and worked as a bartender at the Liar's Club. That was it. Her sister was in love with this man, and whether or not he felt the same way about Nicolette…it was a moot point. Trista wasn't going to hurt Nicolette. She would follow through with her plan and start getting ready to move to New York. Florida had never been a long-term thing anyway. She needed to put a thousand miles between herself and Riker.

Happy with her decision, Trista eased out of bed. Throwing on a robe, she opened her blinds and peered outside. The sky was an angry mix of purple and grey, and the waves were at least three-feet high, throwing foamy water onto the beach. A storm was definitely brewing.

"Oh my God, my head. Why do I drink so much when I know the next morning I'll be paying for it?" Nicolette asked as she saw Trista coming down the back stairs to the kitchen. "Thank goodness I don't have to work today."

"It's just as well. Have you seen the weather?" Trista asked as she walked by, grabbing a mug from the cupboard.

"It's Florida. One minute it's raining and the next the sun is out. It'll blow over soon." Nicolette made herself another cup of coffee. "I made some eggs and bacon."

"I'm good, thanks. Just coffee."

"Where did you slip off to last night?"

The question made Trista stop in her tracks. She wasn't sure how to answer it. Did Nicolette see Riker follow Trista last night? "What do you mean?"

"I saw you leave the party and head down the beach."

Trista turned her back on Nicolette, stalling for time to think about her response, and concentrated on selecting a pod of coffee from the rack. Nicolette had stocked up on all kinds of K-cups, including a mix of flavored coffee. Trista selected a hazelnut breakfast blend, sticking it in the coffeemaker's contraption. "I needed to clear my head and get some fresh air. A walk on the beach usually helps."

"Did you get to know James?"

Trista paused. That was a loaded question, for sure. She'd gotten to know Riker inside and out. But, she didn't think Nicolette had seen her having a rendezvous with her so-called boyfriend. They had been situated a pretty good ways down from the beach house and covered by the sand dunes. "Um, yeah. A little. Why do you call him James? I noticed everyone at the party seems to know him by Riker."

Nicolette shrugged. "I dunno. I think calling someone by their last name is…kinda high schoolish. I think James is more fitting."

Trista couldn't disagree more. Riker was a perfect fit. He was unlike any other man she'd ever met. Most guys she knew who went by James—instead of Jim or Jimmy—were usually the nerdy types. Leave it to her sister to try to change someone into something they weren't.

"I saw you two walking up from the beach last night. I figured he would try to win you over with his charm and quick wit." Nicolette stared at her sister over her coffee mug. It was making Trista very nervous. "What do you think?"

Trista wasn't sure where this was going. So her sister did see them walking on the beach. Did Nicolette suspect something? "Think about what?"

Nicolette sighed. "Wake up, Trista. What did you think about my boyfriend?"

"Uh, I think he's a nice guy."

"So…what did you guys talk about?" Nicolette asked impatiently.

Trista didn't know how to answer that question either. It was too damn early in the morning for this kind of interrogation from her sister. Remembering their beach rendezvous, they hadn't done a whole lot of talking. "We ran into each other on the beach. He didn't say too much. He…" Shit, what should she say? "He said you two had known each other for a while."

"Well, we've had our ups and downs, but I think he's coming around. Riker is one of those types who's hard to nail down." Nicolette scooped some egg onto her fork. "He has commitment issues. But seriously, what guy doesn't?"

"Are you two dating exclusively?" Trista wanted to hear her sister's side. For all she knew, Riker was lying to her. Maybe he had a ton of girlfriends on the side. He was a very handsome and charming man. Somehow she doubted he had lied to her though. He seemed genuine and caring. But, she thought the same thing about her ex-fiancé, Blake, when she had first met him. "I mean, let's face it. You've had some commitment issues yourself."

Nicolette laughed. "Let's just say my Facebook status says 'It's Complicated.'"

"All your past relationships have been complicated." Trista said. *Especially with me.* "But are you in love with him?"

"Did you not see James? He's yummy and he's sweet and he's everything I've ever wanted in a man. Who wouldn't fall in love with all that?" Nicolette spread butter on her toast.

Trista couldn't disagree with her. Riker was yummy. She was feeling so guilty. What the hell was wrong with her? She wanted to mend her relationship with her sister, not tear it apart. From now on, no more trysts with Riker. "But are you *in love* with him?"

Nicolette gave a small shrug. "I could be, I guess."

"So what's the problem? I mean, besides both of your commitment issues." Trista took her coffee and stood across the kitchen counter from her sister. She watched as Nicolette took a bite of toast then pushed her plate away. Her dark hair was a tangled mess and hanging in her face.

"What's with all the questions? You're suddenly interested in my love life?"

Trista sipped her coffee slowly, staring at her sister over her mug. "I want to catch up on everything I've missed the last couple of years." And I want to know how serious you are with Riker because I'm totally fascinated with him. I can't stop thinking about him. She kept that part to herself, obviously.

"Honestly, I have no idea," Nicolette finally answered. "We dated off and on for a year. We've broken up and gotten back together so many times I can't keep track of whether we are off or on," she laughed. "Last month James asked me to meet him for dinner. I thought we were celebrating our anniversary. He even booked a reservation at Edward's in Rosemary Beach. Instead of being a celebration, he said he wanted to date other people."

"Ouch," Trista replied.

Nicolette rolled her eyes. "James needs some time. He knows we are good together. I'm willing to wait until he comes around."

Trista put her mug down. "I'm sure it will all work out. Look, Nicolette, I wanted to talk to you about my plans. I'm not planning on staying in Blue Mountain Beach for long. After breakfast, I'm calling my agent to see if she can line me up some auditions."

"You're going back to California?"

"No, New York. I'd like to give Broadway another shot. You know, a lot of film actresses have gone back to Broadway. It couldn't hurt."

"Now it's my turn to ask the questions." Nicolette studied her sister. "Why did you come back Trista?"

"After I got fired and things went south with Blake, I couldn't think of anywhere else to go. I knew I needed to get out of Hollywood." Trista walked to the sink and rinsed out her mug. "I know things aren't great between us, but I would like a chance to fix that. You know, before I leave."

Nicolette drummed her perfectly manicured fingernails on the countertop. "There has been so much that has happened. I don't know how you think we can repair our relationship in only a few short days."

Trista turned to face her sister. "I don't know how either, but I'd like to start."

Nicolette stared into her empty coffee mug.

"How about this? I'm going to take a shower and change. Let's go shopping and have lunch. My treat. We can talk it over," Trista offered.

"All right," Nicolette agreed. "Give me forty-five minutes. I desperately need another cup of coffee and an aspirin before we go."

Chapter Nine

Trista twisted the handle to HOT and began to fill the Jacuzzi tub. She added a lavender bath bomb and Epsom salts to the steaming water and gently stepped in. If she was going to spend the day with Nicolette shopping, she needed to ease her achy muscles. Between driving for three days straight and her trysts with Riker, Trista was sore all over. Plus, she needed to think things through before she had a conversation with her sister. Nicolette needed to know about Riker. Trista wasn't going to leave Florida without her knowing the full truth. If they were going to repair their relationship, Trista wanted to start fresh with no lies or secrets. She needed to figure out how to approach the subject.

Trista couldn't even remember what really had started the argument between them. She eased her head back on the edge of the tub, closed her eyes, and thought back to the beginning…how it all started.

***

When Nicolette Ricci was six years old, her father had an affair with Trista's mother, Charlotte Carmichael. They all lived in a small beachside town called Coral Cove, which was located a few miles outside of Tampa, Florida. Charlotte was fresh out of college and an intern at Coral Cove Real Estate and Development, which Nicolette's father owned. Sam Ricci was a handsome man who had troubles keeping his pants zipped. He loved the ladies as much as he loved a good deal.

Sam owned one of the largest real estate companies in Florida, with several investment properties all around small coastal towns in Florida. Sam toured around Florida, snatching up deals wherever he went. He was touted in his field of business as a visionary. He took his beautiful intern, Charlotte, on a business trip to Blue Mountain Beach in the late 1980's. There he met a gentleman who had several acres of beachfront property for sale. Charlotte fell in love with the soft, white sands, sparkling turquoise waters, and unencumbered land. She knew Blue Mountain Beach wasn't just another small coastal town. It had charm, it was quiet, and the beaches were virtually untouched. Charlotte encouraged Sam to buy the investment property.

Two months after their visit to Blue Mountain Beach, Charlotte found out she was pregnant. Sam was furious and wanted her to have an abortion. The last thing he needed was a scandal. Charlotte refused. She wanted the baby more than life itself. Sam gave Charlotte money and sent her away to have the baby. There were already rumors floating around about his indiscretions. He didn't want his wife to find out about his bastard baby. Charlotte fled to California where her baby girl was born. She named her Trista Samantha Carmichael. Charlotte tried desperately to reach out to Sam, but he continued to push her away, although he never failed to send her a check every month to take care of her and Trista. Two thousand dollars arrived the first of the month like clockwork. When Trista was three years old, Charlotte died of an accidental drug overdose. She had never recovered from her broken heart and had used drugs to numb her pain. Before she died, she sent a letter to Sam's wife, Marla. In the letter, she told Marla about her affair with Sam…and the baby. In the letter, she explained the child had no other family to take care of her, if something were to ever happen to Charlotte.

When Trista was old enough to understand what had happened, she thought her mother knew she was going to die and always wondered if it was suicide that took her mother instead of an accidental overdose. It was an unanswered question that would always haunt Trista.

Marla received the letter and confronted Sam about the affair. He finally admitted he was Trista's biological father. Marla convinced Sam to fly out to California, where Trista was currently in foster care, and bring his daughter home. After a paternity test and thousands of dollars in legal fees, the Ricci's arranged for Trista to come live with them. By this time, Nicolette was nine years old, and Trista was almost four. Nicolette had always wanted a brother or sister, and when Trista came to live with them, Nicolette was ecstatic. Unfortunately, it didn't last long.

Nicolette was little overweight as a girl. She had gorgeous, thick, dark hair, an olive complexion, and sparkling, hazel eyes. Although she had a beautiful face, from the neck down, she had her father's genes. Sam was Italian and chunky. Nicolette was what people termed "big-boned." They were always telling her, "If you would only lose fifteen pounds, you could be gorgeous." This only led to her binge eating and terrible diet habits.

Meanwhile, Trista started blossoming into a beautiful girl. She had an athletic build, like her mother Charlotte, and had long shiny hair the color of honey, big violet blue eyes, full sensuous lips, and a perky nose. The only hint of Sam was her coloring. Where her mother was pale, Trista had a darker complexion, which only added to her natural beauty.

When high school had started for Trista, Nicolette became jealous of her sister. All the boys were smitten with Trista, and all the girls wanted to be her best friend.

However, Trista wasn't interested in cheerleading, or dancing, or any of the social activities the popular kids were interested in. She wanted to try her hand at Drama Club. Her English teacher, who ran the Drama Club, encouraged Trista to try out for the upcoming school play. Trista tried out for a smaller role, but surprised everyone when Mrs. Clark gave her the coveted role of Hot Lips in the play *M*A*S*H*. After Nicolette graduated high school, she left for college and decided to go to University of Georgia, where her mother had attended. Trista became closer to Marla while Nicolette was at college. When Trista was a senior in high school, Marla was diagnosed with terminal cancer. She had discovered a suspicious mole on her back and the doctor took a biopsy. The diagnosis: Marla had stage four melanoma. The doctor gave her a few months to live. Trista took care of Marla during her final months, taking her to doctors' appointments, holding her hand during chemo treatments, and fixing her meals.

When Marla passed away, it drove the girls further apart. Nicolette blamed her mother's death on Trista, telling her the cancer had stemmed from stress that her mother endured when she found out about the affair. Sam tried to stay neutral. He hated conflict and didn't like the girl's arguing day and night. He threw himself into his work and tried to avoid any fights.

The night Trista graduated high school was bittersweet. Marla had passed away the week before. Nicolette did not attend her sister's graduation, electing to go back to school after the funeral. Only Sam was there. Trista remembered him hugging her and telling her everything was going to be okay, that Nicolette would eventually come around.

Sam then told her he thought it would be a good idea for them to start fresh. He wanted to move his operations to Blue Mountain Beach, where he had many business interests, including a small real estate office and a restaurant and bar. He was also beginning development on the land he'd bought while Charlotte was with him during their first visit to the area. The land he had bought seventeen years earlier had increased ten-fold in value. New houses and condo developments were popping up left and right, and Sam was eager to cash in on his investments.

While Nicolette went back to college, Sam and Trista moved to Blue Mountain Beach. Sam bought a large gulf-front home, and Trista helped him decorate and furnish the home. She had plans to attend a local community college and major in drama. No one knew Trista in Blue Mountain Beach, and she saw this as an opportunity to start over.

Everything was going well until Nicolette came home for the holidays a couple months after they had settled in. It had been almost nine months since Marla died, and Nicolette was still sullen and mad as hell. Nicolette told Trista she was coming home from college to live with her father. They had a huge fight, with Nicolette blaming Trista once again for her mother's death. She told Trista it was time for her to move on and get out of their lives.

Trista packed her bags that evening and, early the next morning, left Blue Mountain Beach. She left a note for Sam, telling him she thought it was for the best. Nicolette needed time with her father, and having Trista around was only going to complicate things.

With a small inheritance from Marla, Trista moved to New York City. She drove all night long, only stopping once to spend the night in Virginia. Trista made it to the Big Apple and decided to stay with a friend from high school who was attending Julliard.

Immediately, Trista landed a small part on Broadway that lasted a year. The role led to another small part on a daytime soap opera, where a producer from a major network spotted her. He had a TV show that was in development—a role he thought she'd be perfect for.

A week later, Trista Carmichael was on her way to Hollywood. She read for the lead part in *You Only Live Once* and was hired on the spot. It was the stuff dreams were made of.

The show was an instant hit. The cast on the show became like family to her. Quinn Miller was her best friend on the show…and in real life. Shane Babineaux played her love interest on the show, and Cheyenne Young played her neighbor. They were all very tight and saw each other frequently off the set.

Two and a half years after leaving Blue Mountain Beach, she was finally in a good place. She missed Sam though. She also missed her sister, despite all the bad things Nicolette said about her. Sam flew out to Hollywood to see her on a few occasions. On one of those trips, he convinced her to come home for the holidays. Sam told her Nicolette was working as a real estate agent for his company and she was miserable without her sister in her life. Trista agreed to fly home for a few nights, hoping Nicolette would be ready to put everything behind them. This was not the case.

Trista's visit home was a big mistake. Nicolette still harbored ill feelings toward her sister. She gave her the cold shoulder all weekend. The night before Trista left, Nicolette suggested it might be best if she never returned to Blue Mountain Beach. Trista accused Nicolette of being a jealous brat, promptly leaving Blue Mountain Beach and vowing never to return.

***

Trista used her toe to pull the drain in the tub. Thinking about the memories of Marla's death and her troubles with Nicolette made her nauseated. Watching the water swirl down the drain, she thought of the conversation she needed to have with Nicolette. It was time to put all their differences aside and try to repair their relationship. It had been several years since Marla died. That was enough time for Nicolette to heal. Trista thought Nicolette had done a good job of moving on with her life. She was a successful real estate agent, following in their father's footsteps, and she had blossomed into a beautiful woman. There was no reason why she should be jealous of Trista. The only thing Trista was unsure of was how to approach Nicolette about Riker. Telling her sister she had sex with her boyfriend would certainly be a setback.

Trista stepped out of the tub and grabbed a towel from the warming rack. It didn't matter how Nicolette reacted to the news about Riker. She needed to be told. And today was better than any other.

Chapter Ten

"Let me buy the outfit for you," Trista offered to Nicolette. "It looks great on you!" They had finished lunch and were shopping in nearby Seaside. Nicolette was celebrating a big sale that had closed, a five-million-dollar beachfront home, once owned by a famous country singer. She modeled a gorgeous navy pantsuit that complemented her curvy figure.

"I have my own money, Trista." Nicolette picked up a gold brooch from the jewelry counter.

"I know that. I want to do something special for you." Trista thought maybe she was doing it to soothe her own guilt about Riker as well.

"Trista Carmichael?"

Trista turned around at the sound of her name. She spotted a woman holding a bunch of dresses in her hands. "Someone said you were in town! I can't believe I ran into you. I loved you as Molly. So feisty and funny." It was like deja vu all over again.

Word travels fast in a small town. "Thank you." Trista smiled politely, waiting for the woman to ask for her autograph or a picture.

"If you don't mind me asking, how long are you planning on staying?"

"Who knows?" Trista shrugged. She was trying to be polite, but today of all days she only wanted peace and quiet. She studied the woman, trying to figure out whether she knew her or not.

"She was fired from her show," Nicolette whispered to the woman.

"Do you two know each other?" Trista asked, startled by her sister's comment.

"This is Michelle Newhouse," Nicolette introduced them. "I sold her a house last year. Michelle teaches drama at the local high school."

"Nice to meet you," Trista said turning to Michelle. "I wasn't fired, by the way. My contract wasn't renewed. Let's leave it at that."

"Well, they're missing out on some great talent." Michelle handed her dresses to the sales girl. "Can you start a dressing room for me, please?"

"What have you been up to?" Nicolette asked Michelle. "Still teaching those teenagers with raging hormones how to act?"

"Yes, not for the school district. I retired from teaching. I now run my own production company and also head up the Blue Mountain Beach Children's Theatre."

"Really?" Trista asked, sincerely interested. "I'd love to hear more about it."

"We're gearing up for our spring play followed by our summer acting camp. You should see the amount of great talent we have from the kids around here," Michelle said proudly. "Why don't you come by tonight? We're having our first meeting for the spring play." She reached in her purse and pulled out a business card, handing it to Trista.

Trista studied the card for a moment before putting it in her pocket. "I just might do it." She thought it was the perfect thing to occupy her time until she could find a job in New York.

"Nice to meet you, Trista. Hope to see you soon." Michelle headed for her dressing room. "Bye, Nicolette!"

Trista and Nicolette gathered their shopping bags and headed out. "Let's have a glass of wine before we head home. I know the perfect place," Nicolette said.

"Okay," Trista agreed. She slipped inside the passenger seat of Nicolette's Land Rover. While Nicolette drove, Trista checked her emails on her iPhone. She received an email from her agent about a voice-over job for a new commercial. She wouldn't have to leave Florida. A small studio in nearby Panama City Beach agreed to provide the technical equipment and studio space for her.

Trista was in the middle of replying to her agent when Nicolette said, "We're here." She looked up and saw they were parked in front of the Liar's Club.

"What are we doing at this dive bar?"

"This dive bar happens to be partly owned by Daddy, in case you forgot. And it is also where the most handsome man in Blue Mountain Beach works."

"You know, on second thought, I'm really tired. Let's go home. We've got tons of wine there."

Nicolette shut off the car. "Come on. Just for a bit. You can visit your picture hanging on the wall by the restrooms," she said with a chuckle.

Trista grabbed her bag. "Okay." She wasn't too crazy about seeing Riker again. She still needed to have a conversation with Nicolette. However, putting it off another day was looking better and better.

The bar was more crowded this time. Being a little after five o'clock, most of the patrons were getting off work. During the off-season it was a mix of blue-collar workers and business types. Come spring break tourists would overrun the bar. Trista and Nicolette chose seats in the middle of the bar. Riker was working with another bartender, a pretty girl who Trista didn't recognize.

"That's Maya," Nicolette whispered in Trista's ear. "I was worried at first when I found out Riker was working with such a pretty girl. She's part Asian, part Irish."

"She is pretty," Trista agreed.

"He's assured me I have nothing to worry about." Nicolette lowered her voice even more. "She's a lesbian."

"I'd still be worried," Trista commented.

Nicolette playfully punched her sister on the arm. "Thanks for the support, sis."

"I'm kidding," Trista said.

"How are my two favorite people?" Riker greeted them with drinks. "Margarita on the rocks for the blonde," he said, referring to Trista, "and a glass of chardonnay for the brunette."

Nicolette smiled. "We just finished up a round of therapeutic shopping." Nicolette leaned in for a kiss on the cheek from Riker, and he obliged. Trista gave him a warning look to back off when he started to lean in to kiss her. She didn't need any special attention from him in front of her sister.

"How's your day been?" Nicolette asked him.

"Busy as usual." Another patron yelled for Riker to bring him a beer. Riker held up a finger indicating he'd be there in a minute. "Can't talk right now. But I'll be back to check on you in a few minutes."

"Looks like Sam made a good investment in this place," Trista said. "If the bar is this crowded on a weekday in late February, I can't imagine what kind of business they do during spring break and summer."

"Oh, it gets crazy. Double the bartenders plus a staff of bouncers and a valet. Weekends they usually have live music." Nicolette twirled her wine glass around. "Daddy has been trying to buy the lot next door to expand the restaurant and bar and put in a huge parking lot. But the owner is being stubborn. He doesn't want to sell."

"Who owns the lot?"

"Carlton Hathaway."

"Why does the name sound familiar?"

"Hathaway is Dad's nemesis—the other big land owner and real estate guru in the area. And he hates Dad with a passion. Last I heard he wants to put his own restaurant on the piece of land. Daddy says Hathaway doesn't know anything about running a restaurant."

"Well, in all fairness, neither did Dad."

"Yeah, well, he's smart enough to hire other people to run his businesses for him. This guy only wants to piss Daddy off."

Trista remembered when her dad bought the land to build the seafood restaurant and bar. Actually the bar came first. Her father wanted a place to hold his famous poker nights, hence the name: the Liar's Club. The seafood restaurant was an afterthought, a way to cash in on the tourists. The seafood restaurant, Lucky Catch, ended up being an award-winning place run by a talented chef. It was packed every night from May to September.

"There are a lot of people who want to piss him off. I'm sure he's used to it." Trista took a long sip of her drink, relishing the sweet and tangy mixtures swirling around her mouth. "Why don't you find Daddy another piece of land? There are plenty of vacant lots up and down the coastal highway. He can relocate the bar and restaurant."

"Don't you think I've tried? It's not about finding him something else. It's about him winning. Having the upper hand."

"Winning what?"

Nicolette laughed. "You don't understand the way things work around here. That's why Daddy trusts me to handle his business."

Another zing at me. Nicolette would always remind Trista she was Daddy's little girl. Not Trista. Nicolette would never forgive her for intruding on their lives. In her twisted mind, she thought Trista was trying to take her mother and father away from her. When Trista's own mother died, she thought she had no one. She was only three years old, for fuck's sake. She didn't ask to be relocated to Florida with a father who never wanted her – at least at first - and a sister who hated her guts. It was ironic Marla was the only one who truly wanted Trista.

That woman was a saint. To take in the baby of the woman who had an affair with her husband was the ultimate act of forgiveness. She had treated Trista like her own daughter since the day she moved in, loving her unconditionally.

Eventually, Trista and her dad became close. It was more of Marla pushing him to do the right thing, but in the end, Sam became the father Trista deserved, and it's all that mattered to her. Marla was the only mother Trista had ever really known, and she treasured each and every moment she had spent with her. It's what made it so hard for Trista to understand why Nicolette never wanted to pursue a better relationship with her. It really hurt.

"Sorry if I'm seeing the simple solution to this problem. If Hathaway doesn't want to sell, then find someone else who will," Trista reasoned.

Nicolette scoffed. "Let's talk about something else."

"Speaking of Daddy," Trista took another sip of her margarita, "have you heard from him lately?" She hadn't seen her dad since she'd arrived in town. He had been on a 'round-the-world cruise with friends. Trista had one brief phone conversation with him the week she left California. He was happy to hear Trista was staying at the beach house for a while and promised to have dinner with 'his girls' when he got back next month.

"*Heyyyy*…I know you!" a male voice boomed behind Trista, interrupting their conversation. His words were slurred. "You're that gurrrrl…from the offfther…night."

Trista turned to come face-to-face with Crazy Jack. His breath was ripe with whiskey. His teeth were stained a sickening yellow that matched his eyes and the tips of his fingers.

"I'm sorry, I don't know what you're talking about," Trista said. She glanced around the bar for Riker, trying to get his attention. When Riker saw Crazy Jack he walked over to them. Trista breathed a sigh of relief. "We've never met," she told Crazy Jack.

"Of course we have. I never forget a purrrty face. I gots a real good memory…"

Nicolette was watching the exchange with a look of curiosity on her face. If Trista didn't get this guy out of here, Nicolette would start asking some questions—questions Trista wasn't ready to answer. She felt relief when Riker came around the bar and headed toward them.

"Hey, Crazy Jack. Quit bothering the ladies. The boys have a little game going on in the back room," Riker said, grabbing Crazy Jack by the elbow. "Let's go see how much trouble we can get into."

"But…I was jus' trying to talk to the purrrrty lady…" Crazy Jack was saying as Riker led him off.

"Huh, what was that all about?" Nicolette asked after watching the whole scene unfold.

Trista tried to laugh it off. "You know how I always attract the loonies."

"When did you meet Crazy Jack?" Nicolette asked, not willing to let it drop.

"I've never met him," Trista said. Which was technically true. Crazy Jack had been passed out almost the entire time she was at the bar that night. He only woke up for a few minutes while Riker was helping him get safely into the cab. She didn't think he would remember her; they hadn't even spoken to one another. "He probably saw me on the show."

Nicolette laughed. "I don't think Crazy Jack has ever watched *You Only Live Once*, let alone any kind of meaningful television."

"That's not true," Riker said, catching the tail end of their conversation when he returned to the bar. "He's a big fan of *Duck Dynasty*. He seems to think he's kin to Silas."

"Exactly my point!" Nicolette exclaimed.

"Hey, can we get going? I'm not feeling too well." Trista pushed her drink away.

"What's wrong?" Nicolette asked.

Riker also looked at her suspiciously, waiting for answer.

"Headache. I need to lie down for a bit."

Nicolette reached in her wallet to pay the tab. Riker waved her off.

"It's on me, ladies." He kissed Nicolette on the cheek again. "Have a nice night. I'll call you later."

Trista walked out of the Liar's Club feeling like the biggest liar of all of them.

Chapter Eleven

The children's theatre was located in downtown Blue Mountain Beach. It had a small indoor stage with seating for one hundred twenty people. There was also a larger amphitheater with lawn seating for outdoor performances and concerts, which was great when the weather was nice. The beach as a backdrop provided the perfect place to enjoy cultural arts. Trista arrived a few minutes before everyone else. Michelle Newhouse was still in her office.

"Trista! I'm so glad you could make it." Michelle jumped up from her chair and shook her hand. "Let me show you around before the kids get here." Michelle was slim with shoulder-length, dark hair, and brown eyes. She wore blue jeans and a black vintage Van Halen t-shirt. Michelle was one of those natural beauties who didn't need to wear a bunch of makeup. Trista guessed her to be in her early forties, but she didn't look a day over thirty. Trista was glad she dressed down for this meeting too. She wore blue jeans paired with a casual peasant blouse and red cowboy boots. Her hair was tied back in a French braid.

As they walked out to the stage, Michelle told Trista the children's theatre relied heavily on donations and yearly fundraisers. "This area was sorely missing an outlet for children to express their creativity. When I knew I was going to retire, I started planning for this."

"What a great idea," Trista said enthusiastically.

A few of the kids arrived, and Michelle had them sit quietly on the stage while she finished speaking with Trista. "As I told you earlier, I would love for you to help us—if you're interested, of course. We're doing the *Magical Land of Oz* this year. It's a two-act adaption of the *Wizard of Oz*. I can always use a hand with the scripts and coaching the kids. We have several other volunteers—some you will meet tonight—who help build the sets, design and sew the costumes, and print the programs. With your Broadway experience, I'm sure you'll be a huge asset to our program."

Trista took in all the kids waiting patiently. She remembered being that age and how much she had loved acting. "I have some time on my hands," she said. "I'd love to help."

"Great. We practice twice a week: Tuesdays and Thursdays for one hour starting at four-thirty. Once it gets closer to show time, we'll go to two hours a night and dress rehearsals."

"Sounds like the good old days." Trista laughed.

When it was time for the meeting to begin Trista joined Michelle on stage and smiled when she introduced the kids to her. Trista was surprised when a lot of children recognized her from TV. Michelle started the meeting and handed out a working script. She announced tryouts for the parts would begin on Thursday and explained every kid who tried out would be guaranteed a part, whether speaking or non-speaking. Some kids had an interest in working behind the scenes. During her talk, a few other volunteers walked in and took their seats in the audience.

"Now to introduce everyone to the volunteers who are helping us this year." Michelle stood and addressed the volunteers who had drifted in. "Some are familiar faces from past productions, and we have some new volunteers this year. First of all, most everyone knows Trista Carmichael. She starred in the popular TV show, *You Only Live Once*. Trista, will you please stand up."

Trista stood on stage and waved to the audience. A ripple of whispering ran through the auditorium.

"Most of you may already know Trista has a vacation home in the area. While she is here visiting, she has graciously volunteered her time and will be helping me with casting and coaching. Everyone say hello to Trista."

The kids yelled out a warm welcome to her along with some adults in the audience.

"Thanks, everyone. This is certainly an honor to be working with each and every one of you. I look forward to getting to know everyone." Trista waved before sitting down.

Michelle continued to introduce a few more people as part of the volunteer crew as each one stood and waved to the kids on stage.

"And last but not least, returning for the third year, is James Riker."

Trista whipped her head around. She didn't realize Riker was part of the theatre crew. She caught his eye as he stood and gave a salute to the kids on stage.

"Riker will be heading up our set crew again this year. If y'all remember, he did a great job on the set for *Rapunzel! Rapunzel!* last year as well as helping with costume designs. This man's talents are vast."

That was true, Trista thought, remembering all Riker's talents. Including the ones he had in the bedroom. She tried to concentrate on what Riker was saying.

"Thanks, Miss Newhouse. I'm happy to be back this year, and I'm looking forward to working with these munchkins again."

Trista heard the little girls giggling. She could've sworn she heard some of the moms in the audience swooning as well.

After the meeting was over, Trista headed outside. A small group of parents had gathered next to the parking lot. She had started for her car when Riker approached her. "We meet again," he said. Riker was wearing his typical work uniform of distressed jeans and a black t-shirt. Trista could see the other women checking him out…and probably wondering what in the world Trista was doing talking to this gorgeous man.

"I thought the whole point of our last conversation was that we steered clear of one another," Trista whispered, crossing her arms over her chest.

"Well, darling, I can't help it you show up wherever I am. How was I to know you were going to be here? Besides, you heard Miss Newhouse. This is my third year doing the children's theatre. What do you want me to do? Quit? I couldn't do that to the little guys."

Trista sighed. "Of course not. This only makes it a little harder."

Riker reached out, taking a piece of Trista's hair and twirled it around his finger. "It doesn't have to be hard. Besides, Miss Fancy Pants, I'll be working mostly backstage. You'll hardly even know I'm there."

Riker's touch set off butterflies in her stomach. Oh, she would know he was there. And she knew she wouldn't be able to resist his charms. "I can't do this anymore, Riker."

"I'm having dinner with Nicolette tonight," he said. He was so close to her she could smell his delicious cologne. And the spearmint toothpaste he favored. It was a yummy combination that made Trista want to take him right then and there and do dirty things to him.

"My relationship with my sister is still rocky. If she found out about this, I'm afraid it would be the end," Trista said, speaking low. Some of the kids and parents were still staring and whispering. A few stood off to the side, waiting to talk to her. "Please, don't say anything to her."

"I'm telling her it's over. For good. She needs to know there's no future for us. Ever." Riker whispered in her ear, "You don't have to worry about me spilling our secret."

"I'm worried about you breaking my sister's heart. You know she's in love with you. Or at least she thinks she is."

"It was never my intention to hurt Nicolette. She's a great girl. But even if you weren't in the picture, Trista, I'd still be doing this. She needs to know it will never work between us." Riker reached out and took her hand in his. "We can't change what happened between us. I know you felt it too."

"Do what you have to do." Trista tried to pull her hand free, but he had a tight grip. It irritated her, but at the same time, she felt electricity course through her body. "As long as *you* know…this isn't going to work."

"If you say so." Riker smiled confidently. He released her hand and walked to his truck. She watched him wistfully. It was over between them she reminded herself. Her relationship with her sister was more important right now. And finding a new job that would take her far away from here.

Chapter Twelve

Trista had gone straight home from the children's theater and pulled a bottle of wine out of the refrigerator. She would've preferred one of Riker's delicious margaritas but it was out of the question, for obvious reasons. Instead she picked up a goblet and a corkscrew, and trudged to the third floor. She drew a hot bath in her Jacuzzi tub and added another bath bomb—this time, a sensuous dark-chocolate-and-almond-scented one. Pouring herself a glass of pinot noir, she took a long sip before stripping down. She gingerly lowered herself into the steaming bubbly water.

She hoped Riker was letting Nicolette down easy. The last thing she wanted was for her sister to suspect anything had happened between Riker and herself before she had the chance to explain. Sinking lower in the tub she let her mind wander and tried to focus her thoughts on what she could do to contribute to the children's theatre. But Riker kept popping into her mind. The way his strong arms held her tightly. The intoxicating smell of his heavenly cologne mixed with his own masculine scent. His kisses, which were passionate and electrifying, and his touch, which made her melt into his arms. The way his hips had ground into hers when he pushed himself deeper and deeper inside. The way he whispered her name when he came.

Trista let her hand drift down below the bubbles. She imagined Riker was in the tub with her as she massaged her clit. The bath bubbles were caressing and spreading a delicious warmth throughout her body. In her mind, Riker was spreading little kisses all over her neck while running his hands all over her body, venturing lower and lower until he found her pleasure spot. Teasing her with his fingers, Riker rubbed her clit with his thumb. He then leaned back in the tub and pulled her on top of him. She eased down on his long shaft, feeling every inch of him slide inside of her. He took one of her nipples in his mouth and gently sucked as she rode him. His strong arms on the small of her back, guiding her as she continued to fill herself completely. Trista closed her eyes tightly as an intense orgasm ripped throughout her body. If she couldn't have Riker in person, she thought, she could at least take advantage of his body in her thoughts. She remained in the tub, eyes closed, her thoughts on nothing but Riker. The water was starting to cool as she slipped into the depths of nothingness.

"Trista! Trista! Are you okay?" A voice from faraway invaded her delicious dreams. She felt a hand grip her shoulder. "Jesus! Get up, Trista."

Trista opened one eye and saw Nicolette standing over her. She was wearing a dark-blue dress with a plunging neckline that showed off ample cleavage. Her face had been heavily made up, but she had dark circles around her eyes and her lipstick had been smeared.

"Oh my God! Are you trying to drown yourself?" Nicolette handed Trista a bath towel.

"I must've fallen asleep." Trista wasn't sure how long she'd been out of it. The water had turned cool, and the bubbles had all evaporated, leaving a slimy film in the tub.

"From the looks of it, you passed out." Nicolette held up a bottle of wine that had a small amount left.

Trista climbed out of the tub, wondering how long she had been in the water. She wrapped the towel around her body, noticing her skin looked like a wrinkled old prune. "I'm fine. Where have you been?" she asked, changing the subject. She held her breath, hoping the dinner had gone smoothly, but from the looks of Nicolette, she knew it hadn't. Nicolette had obviously been crying.

"Don't you know?" Nicolette asked with a hint of suspicion in her voice. "Riker told me he ran into you at the children's theatre. I figured he would've told you we were having dinner tonight."

"Now that you mention it, he might have said something about a dinner." Trista stumbled on her words. "Sorry, I'm a little out of it. I guess I did have too much wine. So how was it?"

Nicolette sighed, sitting on the edge of the bathtub. "Take a good look at me. What do you think?"

"I'm not sure," Trista said cautiously. Riker promised not to reveal anything about their trysts. Had he kept his promise? She proceeded with caution. "Did he hurt you?"

Nicolette shook her head. "He said we were over and it was never going to work between us. I don't know what went wrong. What did I do?"

"Is that all he said?"

"He kept saying he wasn't ready for a commitment and I deserved much better. You know the typical breakup excuses, but usually it's *me* giving them out," Nicolette sobbed. "Not the other way around. The first time I truly give my heart away…look what happens!"

"I'm sorry, Nic." Trista gave her sister a hug. "I know this doesn't help right now, but it will get better. Just take it one day at a time." She plucked a tissue from the bathroom counter and handed it to Nicolette along with the bottle of wine.

Nicolette blew her nose loudly before draining the rest of the bottle. "You know what I think?"

Trista held her breath.

"I think he's seeing someone else. What other reason would he have for breaking up with me? There has to be someone." Nicolette tapped her long, coral-colored nails on the bathroom tile.

"Maybe he's telling the truth. Sometimes things don't work out. He's obviously not the one for you if he can't see the wonderful qualities you have."

"Come on, Trista. Let's face it. There are a ton of beautiful women in Blue Mountain Beach. Hell, half of them frequent the Liar's Club just to flirt with Riker. There has to be someone else." Nicolette fiddled with her tissue. "How could I not see this coming? I know *who* it is…" She glared at her.

Trista sucked in a deep breath. Shit. Shit. Shit. She knows. "Listen, Nicolette. I can explain—"

"Constance Smith!" Nicolette interrupted.

Trista blew out a breath. "What? Who is that?"

"She's the man-eating whore who has been in the bar every time I go in there."

Trista grabbed her robe from the hook and put it on. She tried to remember where she had heard the name before. "Isn't Constance Smith a forty-something divorcee with three kids? Her ex is the plastic surgeon who's on every billboard between here and Panama City Beach, right?"

"Yeah, she's a cougar, all right. And I heard she recently broke up with her twenty-year-old boyfriend."

"I don't see Riker falling for Constance or anyone like her." Trista took the empty wine bottle from her sister's hands. "I know what will make you feel better. Why don't we have a girl's getaway? My treat."

"Really? Where?" Nicolette balanced herself against the bathroom counter to pull off her shoes.

"My friend Quinn is coming in town next week. She mentioned going to the Bahamas. We'll have fun, and you'll soon forget about Riker."

Nicolette walked out of the bathroom, following Trista into her bedroom. "I'll think about it. Until then, I'll be in my room, hibernating under the covers."

Trista closed the bedroom door after Nicolette left. She sat on the edge of her bed and noticed her cell phone blinking. She entered her password and saw she had several missed calls and one text message from Riker.

"*CALL ME MISS FANCY PANTS*."

She erased the message without another thought.

Chapter Thirteen

"What time does our plane leave again?" Nicolette asked her sister for the third time.

"Seven-thirty." Trista took a bite of her bagel. She was getting excited about the prospect of going to the Bahamas for a long weekend. Quinn Miller was flying in town today from LA. Trista was looking forward to spending some quality time with her best friend.

"We should take Quinn out to dinner tonight. Maybe hit up the new club the opened in Destin last month," Nicolette suggested. She was stuffing files into her briefcase, getting ready to leave for work. After a few nights of crying, three pints of Ben & Jerry's ice cream, and several bottles of wine, Nicolette seemed to have Riker out of her system. And if not, a trip to the Bahamas would definitely help.

"I don't think that's a good idea. We have an early flight. I don't know about you, but I don't like flying when I'm hung over," Trista responded. She finished her breakfast and put her plate in the sink. She was glad Lupe, their housekeeper, was coming in today to clean and restock the refrigerator. Not only was the house a complete wreck, but also Nicolette had ransacked the refrigerator. After her breakup with Blake, Trista had done the complete opposite. She couldn't eat for days.

"Don't be such a wuss. It will be a great kick-off to our girl's weekend trip. Besides, Wednesday night is Ladies Night, and this club is supposed to be crawling with cute guys. Who knows, maybe you'll finally meet someone too!"

"I'll think about it." Trista looked at the clock on the microwave. "Don't you have a closing this morning?"

"Shit," Nicolette grabbed her coffee mug and briefcase off the counter. "I didn't realize it had gotten so late. I have to be in Panama City in twenty minutes."

"Then you better hurry." It was the first of March, and spring break had already started in full force, with MTV setting up in their usual spot: Panama City Beach. Traffic would be hellish by ten o'clock.

"What are you doing today?" Nicolette asked, heading for the garage door.

"Laundry. Packing." Trista thought about calling her agent too. Checking in to see if she had lined up any auditions for her. "Then I'm off to the studio to finish the voice-over work before I have to pick up Quinn from the airport."

"Have fun! I'll see ya tonight!" Nicolette slammed the door shut behind her. Trista heard the garage door go up and Nicolette's car rev to life. The garage door eased down a couple minutes later. Now she was all alone in the beach house. Thank goodness. She loved her sister, but sometimes Nicolette could grate on her last nerve.

Trista had a couple hours before she had to be in the studio. She glanced at her phone. For once it was silent. Ever since the night Nicolette came home from her dinner with Riker, Trista had managed to stay away from him. He'd called and texted her for a week straight, but Trista ignored all his texts and deleted his voicemails without listening to them. It didn't matter it was over between him and

Nicolette. She was never going to see him again. She hoped eventually he would get the hint.

Trista started cleaning up the kitchen, putting the rest of the breakfast plates and mugs in the kitchen sink. The housekeeper would be here soon. Nicolette always chided Trista for cleaning up every morning before Lupe came to clean. "Why do you always clean before Lupe gets here? You do know it is her job to do that?" she asked her one morning while Trista was sweeping. She'd answered, "I don't know. I like to tidy up." But she guessed she was used to picking up after Blake. *Old habits are hard to break.* She headed upstairs to get ready for work. In less than ten hours, Quinn would be here, and she could leave her thoughts of Blake and Riker behind her.

Quinn was waiting in the baggage terminal area when Trista got to the airport. Trista spotted her friend immediately. She was the only five-foot-ten, brunette woman wearing a black jumpsuit with bright-red high heels, which made her tower over six feet. Her hair was held back with a sequin headband and hung all the way down to her derriere. Quinn was wearing shiny, two-carat diamond post earrings. Men were enthralled by Quinn's beauty, and women were intimidated by her. Quinn was also smart as a whip. She was not only a great actress, but a talented writer as well. She had written several screenplays and got the green light from a studio last week to start production on a new movie.

Trista met Quinn when she first moved to Hollywood. Quinn had been cast in the role as Trista's best friend on *You Only Live Once*. They quickly became best friends in real life, too. Trista trusted Quinn, and she was the only person who knew about her past. Filled with emotion, she called out to Quinn, who was picking up her Louis Vuitton luggage from the baggage carousel.

"Trista!" Quinn shouted.

Trista hugged her friend tightly. "I'm so happy you're here!"

"I've missed you," Quinn said, returning the hug. "Saturday yoga is not the same without you."

"I bet." Trista reached for one of her bags. "Here, let me help you."

Quinn looked around. "What? No limo driver?"

Trista laughed. "This is the beach. We're relaxed and laid back here. No limos, no drivers today." In LA it was customary to take a limo or car service everywhere. Even though Trista had her white Mercedes coup while living in LA, she hardly ever drove it. The studio had a car service on call, and it picked up Trista every morning and took her home at night. When she went out with the girls, they almost always took a limo.

Trista led her friend outside to the parking lot. She had been lucky and got a parking spot right up front. The weather was cooperating too. March was typically the rainy season, but today the temperature was in the low 70s with sunny skies. A slight sea breeze tousled her hair. She loaded Quinn's luggage into her trunk.

"What is the plan for the weekend?" Quinn asked, as they got settled into the car.

"Nicolette wants to take us out for dinner at the Bowery on 30-A. It's a new steakhouse near the beach. Afterward, we're going to a new club. Nicolette's idea." Trista drove out of the airport parking lot and headed toward the highway that would take them down to the beach. The airport was an hour away from her house, but without tourist traffic, she thought she could make it home within forty-five minutes.

"I told her that going to the club may not be the best idea since we have to catch an early flight tomorrow."

"I happen to think going to the club is an excellent idea!" Quinn smiled. "When did you get to be such a fun sucker? It's been awhile since you and I tore up a dance floor."

"You're right! I guess the last time was to celebrate your thirtieth birthday in Cancun."

"After you hooked up with Mr. Asshole, I hardly saw you anymore."

"I know. I'm sorry. I can't believe I was actually in love with him." Trista took a quick look at her friend. "Why didn't you ever tell me how bad Blake was?"

"Honey, I tried. They don't call it rose-colored glasses for nothing."

"There's something I need to tell you." Trista snuck another peek at Quinn. She was staring at her with those inquisitive green eyes that could see through anyone's bullshit.

"I knew it," Quinn said. "You've slept with someone. I recognize the glow."

"How did you know?" Trista asked, already knowing the answer. Quinn was like a Magic 8 Ball and a tarot-card reader rolled up into one. She instinctively knew when Trista had man troubles. She wished she would've heeded Quinn's warning about Blake.

"Who's the lucky guy?" Quinn asked, ignoring Trista's question.

"I accidentally slept with my sister's boyfriend." Trista sighed. "Well, it's complicated. He's not actually her boyfriend. And I didn't know they were dating."

Quinn laughed. "Damn girl! Does trouble follow you wherever you go? How the hell do you *accidentally* sleep with your sister's boyfriend?"

Trista told Quinn everything that had happened—from the night she drove into town and slept with Riker to when she last saw Riker and broke it off with him. "Nicolette had dinner with him last week, and he told her it was over for good. She came home in tears. Neither of us has spoken to him since then."

"But you want to?" Quinn asked, with a sly smile on her face.

"Of course I do! But if I want to keep Nicolette from killing me and tossing my body in the ocean…"

"You obviously have feelings for Riker?" Quinn waved her hand. "Don't even answer. I know you do. I've seen the goofy look on your face before. You're in love with him."

"I never said that. We have a sexual chemistry that can't be denied. But love? After everything that happened with Blake, I'm not so sure I know what love is anymore."

"You love him. I can tell." Quinn tried to stretch out her large frame in the small confines of Trista's Mercedes. "Blake was only your layover. Some people have direct flights to love. And for some people, it takes two, three, or more stops to get to their destination."

"You think Riker is my destination?"

"I think Riker is your destination, your fairytale, your happily-ever-after ending, all rolled into one."

"All this and you've never set eyes on him."

"I don't have to meet him to know how you're feeling. I can tell from looking at you, girl. You got bit by the love bug, and it shows all over."

"What about Nicolette?"

"You guys had a rocky relationship to begin with. Nicolette needs to grow up and stop blaming other people for her problems. There was a reason it didn't work out for her and Riker. And it wasn't you. Tell her the truth when the time is right. She'll get over it. And if she doesn't…" Quinn shrugged, "then move on with your life. Do what makes Trista happy for once."

Trista nodded. She didn't want to hurt her sister. But all Nicolette had done since Trista was a little girl was to make her life a living hell. She never fully accepted Trista as a sister and always treated her like crap.

They continued to catch up on each other's lives until Trista drove up to the beach house. The pool maintenance guy had parked his truck in the driveway. He was wearing board shorts and nothing else. Quinn stared at him as he lifted a long-handled net out of the back of his truck.

"Nice place," Quinn said. "Who's that?"

"Carlos. He's our pool guy."

"Yummy."

"He's barely eighteen. His dad owns the company. He works part-time and goes to college at night." Trista popped open the trunk. "We have plenty of time to meet other men. Please don't accost my pool boy."

"I was thinking he could give me a proper Florida welcome," Quinn laughed as Carlos approached them and offered to help with her luggage.

Trista punched Quinn on the arm. "Cut it out."

"You know I prefer older men," she added, watching the pool boy carry her bags inside the house. "But there's nothing wrong with having a little something with a younger man every now and then."

Trista thanked Carlos, who was blushing by the time he walked out to the pool deck. "Shhhh…don't get the poor boy's hopes up. Besides, there are plenty of older men here. Florida has more retirees in all of America."

"Yeah, it may be true but I like men that still have all their own teeth and don't have to wear a little button necklace they push when they've fallen and can't get up. And speaking of getting it up…"

Trista laughed, opening the door to the kitchen area. "Okay, that's enough. I get your point."

"I can't wait to see what's in store for us tonight," Quinn said, throwing her purse down on the table. Picking up a bottle of tequila sitting on the kitchen counter she said, "Let's get this party started, chica loca."

Chapter Fourteen

Club Aqua was a new nightclub located in Destin, which was the nearest town to the west of Blue Mountain Beach. The colorful club was housed in a renovated warehouse, a little over twenty thousand square feet of space sectioned into three parts. The largest part had a large dance floor with a live DJ spinning a mix of pop music infused with techno. There was also a VIP section located on two levels: one behind the dance floor and one on the second level, which was roped off and had a discreet view of the whole club. Another part of the club housed a variety of pool tables, dartboards, and poker tables. A long, U-shaped bar served a variety of drinks and appetizers. It was quieter than the other side of the club and had more of laid-back beach theme with pop/country music playing from the stereo system.

"This isn't anything like the Liar's Club," Nicolette mused as they pulled into the parking lot. "I've been trying to get Daddy to open a nightclub like this near Blue Mountain Beach. We need more than just hole-in-the-wall establishments that cater to people like Crazy Jack."

"I had a sneaky feeling this was more than a girls night out at the club. This is a research trip for you, isn't it?" Trista asked her sister. She knew Nicolette was her father's right-hand woman when it came to business dealings. She had to give her sister credit. Nicolette had made

Sam Ricci a lot of money; she was a natural in knowing a good real estate investment when she saw it.

"Consider this a perk of the job," Nicolette said, stepping out of the car. She was dressed in a black leather mini skirt with a white sheer blouse and black high- heel boots. A group of men were getting out of their car at the same time, and all of them turned to stare at Nicolette. She gave them a half wave and smile before turning her attention back to Trista.

Trista took a moment to adjust her dress before getting out of the car. She had decided on the aqua-colored chiffon dress she had bought from the Beach Peach during her last shopping spree with Nicolette. It was a short dress with the hemline hitting a few inches above her knees. The neckline was covered in delicate lace and the back of the dress was open all the way to the middle of her back. It was pretty in the front and sexy in the back. The color of the dress complimented her hair and tan that she still maintained by going to the tanning salon every week. "I'm ready. Let's go," she said to Quinn who was getting out of the backseat.

Quinn was a stunning beauty as always. Trista always joked that Quinn could wear a paper sack and make it look fashionable. Tonight was no exception. Her friend went with an understated look with faded low slung Levis, a cropped white t-shirt that showed off her amazing abs, a black leather studded vest, and a million dollars in diamonds between her ears and navel. She borrowed a pair of rusty-red cowboy boots from Nicolette that added a touch of flair to her outfit. Her long, raven hair hung loosely in a fishtail braid down the right side of her shoulder. Thick, dark eyelashes coated in jet-black mascara made her emerald green eyes pop. The mascara, black eyeliner, and ruby-red lipstick were the only makeup Quinn wore.

"We're counting on you to round them up for us," Trista said to Quinn. She knew as soon as they walked into the club the men would be fighting to talk to her best friend.

"Just remember to save some for me," Nicolette joked.

The three of them made their way inside the club. Nicolette knew the bouncer, and he escorted them to the first-floor VIP section, where a table was waiting for them. While the outside of the club looked like a worn-down piece of crap, the inside was fabulous. The dance floor was made of acrylic glass and had an aquarium underneath. While dancing, you could view all kinds of marine life swimming around, including a few nurse sharks and stingrays. There was stadium-style seating in one section where patrons had a good view of the dance floor and stage. Oversized stuffed chairs and couches were scattered behind the dance floor. In the VIP section, bottle service, tapas, and a personal bartender and waitresses paid close attention to a patron's every need.

The girls sat at one of the tables and ordered drinks. Quinn insisted on starting the night with bottle service and ordered Silver Patron for shots all around. As predicted, it didn't take very long for the men to start lining up at the VIP section, wanting to meet Quinn. The bouncer did a good job of keeping them at bay, only letting in VIP members.

"To hell with this boring VIP stuff. I'm going dancing," Quinn said after downing her shot and chasing it with a beer. She grabbed Trista's hand. "Let's go have some fun, girls."

Nicolette flipped her hair over her shoulder. "I'm staying here." She looked over at the next table where the group of men from the parking lot had been seated. "I see someone I'd like to talk to."

Trista looked concerned for a moment. She realized she and Nicolette had never really gone out like this before and wasn't sure about leaving her big sister alone with a bunch of men neither of them had known. "Are you sure?"

Quinn tugged on Trista's arm. "She'll be fine. Mr. Arms-Bigger-Than-His- Ass over there will protect her if needed," Quinn said, referring to the bouncer assigned to the VIP room.

They hit the dance floor as soon as Miley Cyrus's *Wrecking Ball* remix started playing. Quinn and Trista stood in the center of the dance floor and gazed at the multitude of colorful fish that swam below.

"I've got to say I'm fucking impressed! There is nothing like this in LA," Quinn said, staring at a large nurse shark that circled around before darting off.

"Oh, LA has its share of sharks and barracudas. You've met Gil Salmon, right?" Trista laughed. She knew they were catching the attention of men hanging around the bar. It wouldn't be long before one of the admiring men came hitting on them.

"Gil is a prick who doesn't know his asshole from his elbow. He made a huge mistake by firing you from the show." Quinn took Trista by the hand and twirled her around the dance floor. "Don't you worry your pretty little head. Some fantastic show will come along and scoop you up."

When Trista had found out she had been axed from the show, and after the Blake cheating fiasco, Quinn was the first person who showed up at her front door to console her. She'd told Trista she had no idea Gil was changing up the show and Trista's contract was not being renewed. Apparently nobody did, except for top brass. The rest of the crew showed up later that night, and they all had a drunken three-day weekend, vowing not to return to the show unless Trista was re-hired. In the end, Trista told her co-stars and crew not to cause problems, even though the thought of everyone boycotting the show on her behalf made her heart swell with love for them. Marla used to tell her every dark cloud had a silver lining, and this was one of those times when Trista truly believed something good was going to come out of this. She only wished it would hurry up and get there!

"I hope you're right," Trista yelled over the music. "Watch out. Here come some of your admirers." They looked over at two men heading their way. Barely catching their names over the loud music, Quinn and Trista started dancing with them.

Trista thought her dance partner was cute. He had a nice smile and an even nicer butt that she noticed when he turned around. Quinn's dance partner looked like he could pass for Channing Tatum. *Some girls have all the luck.*

After a few songs, her partner led Trista off the dance floor. They walked back to the VIP section, leaving Quinn and her man still dancing. It was a little quieter in this part of the club, and Trista could finally talk to her dance partner without yelling. A quick look over at the other tables, and Trista saw the three men from the parking lot surrounding Nicolette. She was laughing and looked like she was having a good time.

"My name is Bruce," her dance partner told her. "I wasn't sure you heard me out there."

"Trista Carmichael," she said, holding out her hand.

"Holy shit!" Bruce exclaimed. "I thought you looked familiar. What are you doing here?" He stammered. "I mean, here…not the nightclub. In Florida?"

"Visiting family." It was the safe answer she gave most people. And it was true.

"I love your show," Bruce gushed. "I've watched every episode. Some more than once. Your character Molly is so funny."

Trista smiled. Obviously Bruce didn't read *OK! Magazine*. He thought she was still working on the show. She didn't have the heart to correct him. Bruce was being so cute…and fan boyish. "Thank you. Would you like something to drink?"

"I'm sorry," Bruce blushed. "I sound like some crazed fan, huh? I can assure you that I'm not a serial killer or anything."

Trista laughed. "It's okay. As long as you don't ask me to autograph your ass or anything."

"Would you? Autograph my ass, that is?" Bruce laughed at the expression on her face. "Just kidding. Let me buy you a drink instead?"

The waitress came over at the table. "We already have a tab open, and it'd be my treat. What would you like?" Trista asked, smiling at the waitress who was waiting for their order.

"If you insist. Crown and seven, please."

"I'll have another margarita." She waited for the waitress to leave. "So, what do you do?" Trista asked Bruce.

"I'm a lawyer. Family law, real estate closings, some malpractice and personal injury. A little of everything."

"Living in a small coastal town I would imagine you have to diversify, huh?"

"Yeah, something like that. I hate to bore you to death about law. I bet your life is way more exciting."

Trista thought about her cheating fiancé, losing her job on the show, and having sex with her sister's boyfriend. It was then she realized her life sounded like a real-life soap opera. "I guess you can say that."

They continued to talk. The more they did, the more Trista liked Bruce. After his initial fan crush, she realized Bruce was a funny guy. And he wasn't bad to look at. His facial features were rather plain, but he had beautiful blue eyes and a nice body. He wasn't egotistical like most men in LA and wanted to know more about her rather than spending time talking about him. He seemed like a true southern gentleman—he was originally from Georgia and had moved to the beach to take care of his ailing mother, who had recently died of MS. Trista told him about her own stepmother's battle with cancer. She realized they had a lot in common. As the next couple hours flew by, she became more entranced with Bruce. He leaned over and kissed her. His lips were nice and soft, and the kiss was sweet. It wasn't passionate like she had with Riker. But she didn't mind.

"I'm sorry. Was that too fast?" Bruce asked.

"No, actually it was really nice." Trista looked around to check on Nicolette. But she wasn't in the VIP section anymore. The club was getting crowded wall-to-wall with people, and she couldn't find Nicolette or Quinn anywhere in the madness. It made her very nervous not knowing where they were. "Sorry, I think I need some fresh air. Would you excuse me for a sec?"

"Would you like some company?" Bruce offered.

"Um, sure." Trista said. "Let me find my friends, and I'll meet you by the front door."

"Okay," Bruce agreed. He leaned in and gave her another kiss. This time on the cheek. "See ya soon."

Trista headed for the dance floor, but Quinn wasn't among any of the dancers. She turned to check the bar when she felt a hand on her shoulder. A familiar handsome face stared back at her.

"Riker! What are you doing here?" Trista yelled above the loud music.

"I'm with some friends from work," he answered. "What's up with you and nerdy boy?"

Trista's eyes widened. Had he been watching her this whole time? "He's not a nerd. What are you doing? Stalking me?"

"I happened to be walking by the VIP section when I saw you two snuggled on the couch. Did you meet this guy tonight?"

Trista put her hands on her hips. "I'm not going to discuss my personal life with you. It's really none of your business."

Riker put his hand on her elbow. "Let's go somewhere quiet where we can talk about this."

Trista tried to jerk her arm free, but he held a tight grip on her. "I don't think so," she said between clenched teeth.

"Five minutes, Trista."

Trista stared at him for a moment, taking in his gorgeous eyes and the deep dimples that never failed to cause her to swoon. He was too damn irresistible. Where was Quinn when she needed her? Trista felt her resolve melt away. "Okay. Five minutes. That's it." She forgot all about Bruce as she followed Riker through the crowded nightclub. They passed the bar area where she finally spotted Quinn sitting with the same guy she had been dancing with. They were throwing back some shots and laughing. She looked around for Nicolette again but didn't see her.

Riker continued to hold her hand as they passed the restrooms and the stairs, which led up to another level that housed the DJ booth. Another set of stairs was roped off and held a sign marked PRIVATE. Riker removed the rope and held it open for Trista. She thought about asking him where they were going, but she knew he would ignore her. She passed through and waited until he put the red velvet rope back in place. They quickly made their way up. It was darker there, and Trista stopped, waiting for her eyes to adjust. Riker grabbed her hand again and led her to a leather couch that was pushed against a wall. Once they were seated, Trista could see they were in another part of the club, similar to the VIP section. "What's this?"

"The owner reserves it for private parties. We're in luck. No parties tonight."

"I take it you're friends with the owner?"

Riker nodded. "You could say that."

Several other seating areas held a variety of chairs, tables, and couches. A few potted plants were scattered around. It was peaceful up here, away from the crowds and loud music, although Trista could still feel the vibrations of the bass through the floor.

"Now, tell me what you're doing here with that guy." Riker put his arm around Trista as he leaned back on the couch.

"I'm not here with Bruce. My friend Quinn is in town, and Nicolette and I decided to take her out tonight."

Riker nodded. "You kissed him."

"Yeah, so?"

"I didn't like it."

Trista laughed. "We aren't dating, Riker."

"Doesn't matter. I still don't like you being with other men."

"Well, get over yourself. I can kiss whomever I damn well please!" Trista started to stand, but Riker grabbed her and pulled her on top of his lap. As she turned toward him, Riker planted his lips firmly on hers. His tongue met up with hers, as they playfully teased each other.

He tasted delicious, and she started to feel the familiar ache bubbling up. If she didn't get up and leave now, she wouldn't be able to hold back any longer. She felt his hand snake up her dress and rub against her white lacy thong. "You're already wet," Riker whispered in her ear. "I knew you missed me."

"Why do you do this to me?" Trista groaned.

"You like it," Riker answered, inserting a finger in her panties, finding her clit. He gently applied pressure, causing Trista to suck in a deep breath. She could feel his mounting erection through his designer jeans. Within seconds, she had completely forgotten all about Bruce.

***

Trista walked out of the bathroom stall and washed her hands in the sink. She looked up when she heard someone call her name.

"Trista! Who was the hottie I saw you with?" Quinn asked, walking into the bathroom. "And what happened with the other guy? He's been looking for you!"

Trista looked around for Nicolette to see if she had followed Quinn to the bathroom. She pulled her favorite lip-gloss out of her purse and swiped it on her swollen lips before responding, "He's just a friend."

"Bullshit!" Quinn said, standing right next to Trista. Leave it to her best friend to see right through her lies.

"Where's Nicolette?" Trista asked.

"She's at the bar waiting for us," Quinn said. A slow smile crept across her face. She leaned in and whispered, "That was Riker?"

Trista smacked her lips. "Yeah."

"He's so fucking hot. No wonder you're worried. I would beat your ass if I were your sister."

"Yeah, I know" Trista repeated, running a hand through her hair, trying to undo the tangles Riker had put there by wrapping his fingers around the strands while she fucked him. "Now you see my dilemma."

"You had sex with him, didn't you?" Quinn grabbed Trista by the hand, turning so they were face-to-face. "Oh my God, you did!"

A slow smile crept across her face. Trista said, "It's that obvious, huh?"

"You sneaky little bitch. I want details."

The other women in the bathroom were crowding around them. A couple of girls were staring, trying to figure out who they were.

"Later." Trista put her lip-gloss in her purse, snapping it shut. "Let's go before Nicolette gets all pissy on us."

"That guy is still looking for you."

"Crap. I forgot about him."

"I bet." Quinn quickly reapplied her own lipstick. "Don't worry. I'll find him and tell him you don't feel well. You go get Nicolette. I'll meet you outside."

Trista nodded. She headed to the bar while Quinn went the opposite direction to the VIP section. It had been one hell of a night. She was ready to get on the plane in the morning and head to the Bahamas. She needed this weekend away to figure out what she wanted to do about Riker.

Chapter Fifteen

After Quinn's comment about not getting the royal treatment when Trista picked her up from the airport, Trista surprised Quinn and her sister with a chauffeured ride to the airport. The limo driver picked up the girls at the beach house at four thirty the next morning. With only about two hours of sleep, Trista felt like a jackhammer was drilling into her brain. As the driver loaded their bags into the trunk, Trista, Nicolette, and Quinn settled into the back of the black stretch limo.

"This is a real treat," Quinn said, popping open a bottle of Dom. She took a healthy sip of orange juice then chased it with a gulp of champagne. Trista watched as Quinn repeated the process twice. "The hair of the dog and all that," Quinn said, wiping her mouth with a cloth napkin.

"We have champagne glasses, you know," Nicolette said, pointing to the crystal flutes secured in cup holders.

"Someone is grumpy this morning," Quinn retorted, as she opened her purse and popped out two white pills. She washed them down straight from the champagne bottle, sans orange juice this time.

Quinn had dressed for the flight with black leather pants, a sheer Stella McCartney pink polka dot blouse, and a pair of jet black Jimmy Choo booties. Trista admired Quinn. She looked like she had stepped out of a glossy ad from a Cosmopolitan magazine page. Her best friend was always well put together, no matter how many hours she had slept or how many cocktails she had consumed the night before.

"I only slept for an hour. My head feels like it's going to explode," Nicolette whined. She had dressed similar to Trista—casually—with a lavender Juicy tracksuit and flip-flops. Her toenails were freshly painted with OPI's I Just Can't Cope-a-cabana color, which reminded Trista of a lemon slushy.

Quinn offered Nicolette the bottle of pills. "Vicodin. Cures all hangovers."

"I don't think you should be drinking with those," Nicolette said, eyeing the pills warily.

Quinn shook one out from the bottle and handed it to Nicolette. "I'm a pro, darling." She pulled a bottle of soda from the cooler. "Here. Down the hatch. You'll be feeling no pain soon, I promise."

Trista watched as her sister put the pill in her mouth and swallowed. Nicolette winced as she washed it down with Coke. "I hope this cures my pounding skull."

"It was your idea to go out last night. I wanted to stay home and cook dinner, if you remember," Trista reminded her.

"Nobody likes a know-it-all," Nicolette snapped before shutting her eyes. "Besides, you ended up having *fun*, right? So shut up."

Trista exchanged quizzical looks with Quinn. She was used to her sister's bad moods when they lived together many years ago. However, she hadn't witnessed one like this since Trista had moved back home. Trista hoped Nicolette's mood would get better once they landed in the Bahamas. She had planned on spending some quality time with her sister and working things out between them. Things weren't off to a good start.

Within thirty minutes, the driver was pulling into the airport. Nicolette opened her eyes and peered out the window. It was still dark outside, with only the lights of the runway and parking lot illuminating the area.

"We're at the Destin airport?" Nicolette said, looking at Trista for confirmation. Destin had a small airport that catered to private planes. She had used the airport once before when she flew home for the holidays. A few local celebrities who lived in the area, like Emeril Lagasse, kept their private planes housed here as well.

"Surprise!" Trista said with a little more enthusiasm than she should have, given Nicolette's sour mood.

"I thought we were flying commercial?" Nicolette said, confused.

Trista shook her head. "I splurged and booked us a private jet."

"Now we're talking," Quinn said, smiling brightly. She held up the half full champagne bottle.

Nicolette shrugged. "It's your dime."

As the driver pulled up to the front of the airport terminal, Trista grabbed her purse off the seat next to her. She turned to face Nicolette. "That's right. It is my dime. And if you're going to be in a pissy mood all weekend, maybe you should stay here."

Quinn shot her a warning look. She reached inside her purse and pulled out another prescription bottle. This time she shook out three small blue pills and handed one to Nicolette. "No one is staying home," Quinn said. "Take one of these. You'll feel like a new woman by the time we land in Nassau."

Without hesitation, Nicolette popped the pill in her mouth and chased it down the champagne bottle Quinn handed her.

"What the hell are you trying to do?" Trista asked with growing alarm. "I don't want to kill my sister… not just yet."

"Ha ha." Nicolette said smugly. The driver opened the door, and she stepped out first.

"Relax, it's only a little something to calm her down." Quinn grabbed her bag, following Nicolette. "Do you need one too?"

"What the hell? Do you have the whole fucking pharmacy in your purse?" Trista asked, getting out of the limo. She had seen Quinn pop painkillers before. She was known to have legendary migraines, but never had she seen her drink alcohol with them or take them with anything else.

"Just about anything you need." Quinn smiled. Then she saw Trista looked really concerned. "It's okay, relax. I have a prescription for everything. I always take a little something before I fly. You know that."

Trista thought back to the flights she had taken with Quinn before. She was right. She did remember Quinn taking a Valium or Xanax before a flight to Hawaii. And another time when they flew to Europe. It was the norm for some people to have a little something to settle nerves before a flight, so she decided not to make a big deal of it. Trista led them to the airport's check-in lounge, and they waited for the flight crew. A few minutes later, they boarded the plane, and an attractive, female flight attendant greeted them. She got them comfortable and offered drinks and breakfast. Nicolette declined and immediately went to sleep. Quinn and Trista accepted a full breakfast of eggs, waffles, bacon, hash browns, toast, and coffee. While Nicolette slept in the back of the plane, Quinn and Trista sat up front at the table, eating their breakfast after takeoff.

"What exactly did you give her?" Trista asked Quinn. She was dying to talk to her friend about what happened last night with Riker.

Until now, she hadn't had a chance for fear that Nicolette would overhear.

"A Valium. Between that and the painkiller, she'll be out for a while. By the time we get to the Bahamas, Nicolette will be in a much better mood."

"Do you think she knows?" Trista asked in between bites of toast.

"About your secret lover?" Quinn whispered. "I don't think so. Surely she would've said something to you by now?"

Thinking about her sister's bad temper, Trista knew Nicolette wouldn't hold back if she suspected anything between her and Riker.

"Yeah, if she knew what happened last night she would've torn into me by now."

"So tell me. Where did you two go?"

Trista told her about the private area Riker led her to. She also told her about the hot sex on the couch while watching the people dancing below them.

"Ah…a little bit of exhibitionist, huh? *Will we get caught or won't we?*" Quinn smirked. "He's a hottie. Obviously he's good in the sack?"

"Better than good. Hypnotic. Fantastic. Mind-blowing sex."

"Better than Blake?"

Trista scoffed. "No comparison."

"So what's the problem, sweetie?"

"Riker's like a drug. I'm addicted to him. I know being with him is wrong, but he makes me feel all warm and fuzzy on the inside. Ever since I met him, no one else is even worth thinking about," Trista whispered. "Believe me, I've tried. But everything leads back to him. I really think I'm falling hard for him."

Quinn looked at Nicolette, who was still comatose in her seat, and then back at Trista. "Then explain to me why you can't be with Riker if you feel this way?"

Nicolette let out a long snore causing Trista to giggle. "Are you sure she'll be okay? She's drooling.

"Yeah, she's fine," Quinn laughed. "Let her sleep."

Trista continued to watch her sister. "She told me she was love with him. It would kill her to know what happened. That's why I can't be with him."

"She'll get over it." Quinn took her friend's hand in her own. "You deserve to be happy, Trista. If he makes you happy, then so be it. It's really simple."

Trista picked up her fork and toyed with her eggs, pushing them around her plate. "It sounds so simple when you say it, but every time I start to tell her about Riker, I can't get the words out."

"Look, just rip off the Band-Aid. Tell her the truth about what happened. You didn't know who Riker was when you first slept with him." Quinn took a huge bite of hash browns, chewing them slowly before she spoke again. "But for the love of bacon, don't tell her until after the trip. I don't want to play referee the whole time."

Trista took another glimpse at her sister sleeping peacefully and nodded. She would do anything for her, despite all the bitterness that lay between them. "I'll find the right time to do it when we get back."

"Atta girl! Now, let's talk about all the fun we'll be having in a couple of hours."

Chapter Sixteen

"After three days of lying in the sun, shopping, and eating in fabulous restaurants I'm going to be absolutely worthless when we get home tonight," Trista said while they waited on their drinks at Senor Frogs. The famous restaurant and bar was crowded as usual with tourists and cruise-ship vacationers. They managed to get a table overlooking the beautiful Caribbean, instead of a view of the cruise ship docks. Trista watched a few rowdy customers having fun doing a conga line, and the waitresses pouring shots for everyone who passed by them.

"This little vacation is just what I needed," Quinn agreed. "I haven't had this much fun since we went to Mexico."

"I think I gained five pounds since we've been here." Nicolette reached for her drink the second the bartender set it down. It was her third strawberry daiquiri in the last hour.

"Vacation pounds don't count," Quinn responded, drinking her own Red Stripe beer. Quinn was not a fruity-drink kind of girl. She preferred beer, wine, or champagne. The more expensive the bottle, the better she liked it.

"Humph." Nicolette slurped her drink. "Tell that to my jeans."

"Let's hit up the straw market on the way back to the hotel," Trista suggested. "I want to buy something for my dad."

"Good idea," Quinn agreed. "I need souvenirs to bring the crew."

Trista tried to hide her hurt feelings. She knew Quinn would return to LA tomorrow and start taping for the new season. A new season of *You Only Live Once*—without her. As much as she tried to avoid the Hollywood rags and entertainment news on TV, she couldn't help but notice everyone had moved on to bigger news. Kim Kardashian's upcoming nuptials to Kanye West had stolen the spotlight lately. Trista guessed it was a good thing. She didn't want to be forgotten so quickly.

"I can't wait to see what bullshit Gil and his team of writers have come up with to explain your absence from the show. They were supposed to email me the latest script, but I still haven't seen it," Quinn said, making a show of checking her iPhone again.

"I already told you he said Molly was supposed to die in an accident," Trista said, a little more defensively than she intended. She took a huge sip of her own drink. A frozen margarita, not nearly as good as Riker's.

"Yeah, but you know how Gil changes his mind. All the fucking time! I really think he likes to see us squirm," Quinn responded.

"We should get something to eat before we catch our flight," Nicolette interrupted. Trista saw her sister kick Quinn on the foot—she was trying to change the subject for her benefit. Maybe there was hope for her and her sister after all, Trista thought, smiling. Nicolette knew Trista had come to the Bahamas to forget all about getting fired from the show and her breakup with Blake.

"Ow, what the fuck?" Quinn looked over at Nicolette. "If you want my attention, just ask."

"I don't think Trista wants to talk about Gil or the show," Nicolette remarked.

Quinn reached inside her purse and dug around. She palmed another white pill and popped it in her mouth.

Didn't she take one an hour ago? "It's okay," Trista said. "With all the paparazzi following us around this weekend it's hard not to think about it.

Quinn said, "Sorry, Trista. I wasn't thinking."

Trista took another sip of her margarita. "Do you have another headache?" She was growing alarmed at the amount of pills her best friend had been taking all weekend. She seemed out of it most of the trip.

"Yeah, it's that time of the month and I've got another migraine brewing." Quinn stood up from the barstool. "Excuse me, I have to go to the restroom."

"She's taking too many," Trista said to her sister as soon as Quinn was out of earshot.

"I thought it was all part of the Hollywood party lifestyle." Nicolette stirred her drink before downing the rest of her red slushy liquid.

"Not for everyone." Trista thought back to her time in LA with Quinn. She never remembered her friend taking so many pills. She would wait until after the trip and say something to her.

"I'm glad we're alone for a bit," Nicolette said. "There's been something I've been meaning to talk to you about."

Trista felt her stomach give a lurch. While she hated confrontation, Trista knew it was time they cleared the air. "Okay? You got my full attention."

"I think it's time for me to move out of the beach house. I'm going to get my own place."

Trista felt relief flood throughout her body. She visibly relaxed her tense muscles in her neck and shoulder. "You know you're welcome to stay for as long as you like. It's your home, too."

When Sam Ricci had first moved his family to Blue Mountain Beach, he bought and renovated a huge beach estate for them to live in. It was the largest estate home in the county with over ten thousand square feet of space. But after Trista left for New York City, he decided to downsize and buy a condo. For the longest time, it was only Trista and her father. The three-bedroom condo on the beach was perfect for them—until Nicolette decided to move back home after college and Trista set out on her own.

When Trista made her first million dollars two years later, the real estate market had taken a huge tumble. Especially in Florida and California. Houses that were once worth millions of dollars could be bought for pennies on the dollar. Her dad convinced her to buy her first piece of investment property. Trista bought the beach house, sight unseen based on his recommendations, for a mere four hundred thousand dollars; the original owners had paid over three million for it in 2001.

Nicolette had offered to live in the house and take care of it while Trista was in LA. Trista wanted desperately to get along with her sister so she'd agreed. Even though their relationship was never the same again, she felt a sense of relief her sister was watching over her investment. Now she wanted to move out.

"I appreciate that." Nicolette pushed her empty glass away. She got the bartender's attention and ordered another. "I really do. But it's time for me to get my own place. I think its part of the reason Riker wanted to break things off."

"Because you live in my house? That's silly."

"Part of the reason he was mad at me was because I didn't tell him about you. That I had a sister."

"He said that?" Trista asked, incredulously. "Why?"

"Well, not in those exact words. He thought I was hiding my past from him. He wanted to know why I never told him about you."

Trista wondered the same thing. Granted they didn't grow up in Blue Mountain Beach. Not many people knew Nicolette Ricci had a famous sister. Trista was curious why Nicolette didn't want people to know they were related. Now was the time to find out. "Why didn't you tell anyone about me?"

Nicolette sighed as she fiddled with her empty plastic cup. "Then it would've made it real. Telling people we were sisters would mean everyone would know about Dad's affair. It almost tore apart their marriage, you know. I still remember the fights, and Mom threatening to kick Dad out of the house. I still remember her crying for weeks because she found out he had a child with another woman. I still remember the way it felt to have your whole family ripped apart. She was really hurt and so was I."

Trista never thought about the pain Nicolette must have went through seeing her parents fight. "I'm sorry…I didn't think about it that way." Now she understood where Nicolette was coming from, although it didn't excuse her bad behavior.

"After Mom died, I took it out on you. I was really mean to you when I shouldn't have been. Things were said that couldn't be unsaid. And I'm sorry for saying those things," Nicolette said as she brushed a tear away.

Trista reached over and rubbed her sister on the back. "It's okay. I know you were hurting. It wasn't easy on you, having a new sister thrust into your life, having to share your parents with someone else."

"That's still no excuse. You're my sister, and I treated you like shit. If I could take it all back, I would."

Trista got a few bar napkins and handed them to Nicolette, who was still crying. "I still don't want you to move. But if you insist, at least let me go house hunting with you."

"It's time I got my own place," Nicolette said, wiping her eyes. "Although I appreciate you letting me live there while you were gone."

"What the hell? I leave you two alone for a few minutes, and now y'all are both a blubbering mess." Quinn stood behind them, smoking a cigarette. She tilted her head toward the sky and blew a ring of smoke. "What's going on?"

"Nicolette is getting her own place," Trista quickly said before Quinn thought it was a discussion about something else. Like Riker.

"Cool," she said, jumping from one foot to the next. "Are you guys ready to jet? We only have a couple hours before we have to leave for the airport.

Trista finished the last bit of her drink. She laid a hundred-dollar bill on the bar to take care of their check. "Let's go."

Chapter Seventeen

The rays from the morning sun made their way across Trista's bed and onto her face, waking her up. Lazily, she stretched and inhaled the aroma of coffee. Even three floors up, she could smell the delicious breakfast blend her sister was brewing. Glancing at her bedside clock, she saw it was almost seven thirty. They didn't get in from their flight until after midnight. Trista was surprised her sister was up this early. She usually wasn't an early riser. Grabbing her robe from the bathroom, Trista plodded downstairs to see what Nicolette was up to.

"Are you ready to go?" Nicolette asked, pouring fat-free milk into a huge bowl of Rice Krispies cereal.

"Go where?" Trista mumbled, still not quite awake. She headed straight for the Keurig and started to brew her own cup of coffee. Selecting a K-cup of Jet Fuel, appropriately named for its amount of caffeine, she popped it into the machine and waited.

"I'm looking for a new place today," Nicolette reminded her.

"Oh yeah." Trista looked in the fridge for the coffee creamer, hoping Lupe remembered to buy some. She found a large, unopened bottle of French Vanilla creamer and wrapped her fingers around it. "I didn't know we were getting started at this hour."

"Early bird catches the worm. Or in this case, gets the best deal on a piece of property."

"You sound like Dad." Trista caught the look on her sister's face. "Okay, okay. Can I at least get dressed and drink my coffee?"

"Sure. Make it snappy."

After throwing on a pair of jeans and a black crochet tunic, Trista met her sister downstairs forty-five minutes later. Nicolette was waiting impatiently, briefcase in one hand and iPhone in the other. Trista opened the door that led to the garage and pushed the button for the garage door to open.

"You know you don't have to do this," Trista said for the third time as she scooted in to the passenger seat of her sister's Range Rover.

"I do." Nicolette carefully pulled out of the driveway.

"So what are we looking at today?" Trista took a sip of her coffee, trying to clear the morning cobwebs from her brain. It was her second cup of the morning. She still had vacation brain, and all she wanted to do was sleep.

Nicolette handed her a sheaf of papers from a folder that was hidden between the driver's seat and console. "Three condos and a townhome. Shouldn't take too long. They're all located in Alys Beach."

Alys Beach was a quick fifteen-minute drive from Blue Mountain Beach. Located on the same beach highway, it was known to locals and tourists as "30-A," a thirty-mile stretch of beach highway that started in Dune Allen Beach and ended at Inlet Beach, with over fourteen beach towns in between.

"Does Dad know?"

"What? I'm moving out? Yeah, we talked about it a few days ago." Nicolette gave a quick look at her sister. "Actually, it was his idea."

Trista kept a smile on her face; despite the obvious zinger Nicolette threw at her. Nicolette didn't tell her that when they were in the Bahamas. This being her Dad's idea was a shocker. Why wouldn't he call and talk to her about it?

Nicolette pulled into a complex called Palm Dunes Villas. It was a small row of beachfront townhomes that were off-white stucco with pale-blue roofs. A swimming pool and tennis court were situated to the left of the complex and surrounded by a tall, white fence.

"This is the only townhome complex nearby that has a tennis court. Plus it's a short drive to my office." Nicolette took the file from her sister and exited the car. Trista followed suit. "I know the listing agent. She's a big bitch and is still sore with me for selling a beachfront parcel to one of her former clients, but I think I can get them down on the price a bit. It's been listed for over four months with no offers."

Trista wasn't surprised about Nicolette taking away someone else's client. She was known in the local real estate market as a barracuda, like her father. She watched as her sister sashayed up to the front door, entered a code in the lockbox and retrieved a key. They walked into the villa.

"This unit has views of the gulf from all three levels. The bottom has a guest bedroom and bath. Also a rec room, but I think I'm going to gut it and make it an office." Nicolette turned to face her sister, putting her hands on her hips. "What do you think?"

Trista looked at the worn furniture, the pool table, and foosball game in the center of the rec room. "What about all the furniture?"

"This was a rental, so it's really worn. I'll donate everything to Goodwill." Nicolette ran her hand around the granite countertop that covered a wet bar beneath it. "I'll keep the small kitchenette down here, but get rid of everything else. New paint, flooring, cabinets, and furniture."

Trista nodded and followed her sister to the second level. She was impressed by her sister's ability to take a unit that needed a lot of work like this one and make it into something new and beautiful.

"This level, as you can see, has the kitchen and living room on one end and a master suite on the other. I'm going to gut the kitchen and put in Silestone countertops and a nice tile backsplash. The living room walls need painting. And the master suite I'm going to use as another guest bedroom."

"What about the other two condos we are seeing? It seems like you have your heart set on this place."

"This is my first choice. It's a little out of my price range, but like I said, I think I can get them down some."

"How much?" Trista asked.

"One point six."

Trista knew it would probably be a stretch for Nicolette. She didn't exactly know what her finances were; she knew her sister made good money selling real estate. But she also knew Nicolette put almost all the money she made back into investments. Her money was tied up in real estate, like their father's was. Together, they owned several rental houses and apartment complexes.

"I want to pay cash obviously, and I may have to sell some things to do it." Nicolette started up to the third level. "I think one point one would be a good starting price to negotiate."

"That's five hundred off asking. Think they'll go any lower?"

Nicolette smiled at her sister. "I'm a good negotiator."

The third level held a large open space with breathtaking views of the Gulf of Mexico. It was not unlike Trista's bedroom with floor-to-ceiling windows and a sliding glass door leading out onto a balcony. Four pairs of bunk beds lined the walls, and there was a space currently used as play area with a mounted flat-screen television, a Nintendo Wii system, a bookcase filled with children books, video games, and DVDs. Scattered around the floor were several colorful beanbag chairs.

"I'm going to turn this area into a master suite." Nicolette led her to the bathroom. "The contractor said he could add considerable space to the bath, and we could add a walk-in steam shower, claw foot tub, heated floors, heated towel racks, his and hers vanities, a separate make-up table, and under-cabinet lighting."

"That would be beautiful," Trista said. It was almost the exact spa bathroom she had now. "How much would renovations cost you?"

"Around one fifty."

"One hundred fifty thousand dollars?" Trista asked, balking at the price.

"Right."

"Furniture?" Trista asked.

"I figure another hundred thousand or so."

Trista tried to think of a way she could help without offending her sister. She knew Nicolette wouldn't allow any handouts from her. "Your birthday is coming up soon. Why don't I buy the furniture? Kind of like a housewarming gift plus birthday present?"

"For the whole house?"

"Sure, why not?"

Nicolette chewed on her thumbnail, considering her sister's generous offering. "How about only the downstairs? I'm not even sure what kind of furniture I want to buy yet."

Trista thought it was better than nothing. She really wanted to help her sister, and if buying a few pieces of furniture would help, then it is what she would do. "Okay. Just let me know what you decide."

Nicolette was focused on her iPhone. "There's one more listing I want to show you."

"Why are we looking at another condo? This one is obviously perfect for you. We'll make it happen."

"I want another option if this falls through."

Trista laughed. "It's not going to fall through. You're one of the best real estate negotiators around. Remember?"

Nicolette looked up from her phone and smiled brightly. "You're right." She took another look around at the views from the living room area. "It's perfect for me."

"Write it up," Trista said, following her sister to the front door. "If you need help—"

Nicolette waved her off. "I'm good. How about some lunch?" As soon as Nicolette opened the door, Trista saw a familiar face. Riker was standing by his truck with a tool belt on his waist. He wore a tight white t-shirt that showed every single muscle in his arms and chest. A pair of blue jeans and cowboy boots completed his ensemble. He was sexy without even trying. Their eyes locked immediately.

"James!" Nicolette said, rushing up to him and wrapping her arms around his neck.

He continued to look at Trista over Nicolette's shoulder, giving her a half-smile.

"What are you doing here? I didn't think you could make it." Nicolette hugged him tighter.

"What's going on here?" Trista said, confused.

"Your sister asked me to take a look at this place."

"You're the contractor?" Trista asked, looking directly at Riker. She didn't even realize Nicolette was speaking to Riker again after their last heartfelt dinner, where Nicolette had returned home crying. Apparently everything was kosher between them now.

"Well, I'm…" Riker looked between the sisters, unsure of what he had gotten himself into.

"I asked him to take a look at the infrastructure. See if everything is sound. With houses on the beach, you never know," Nicolette explained. She gave Riker a quick kiss on the cheek. "We're going to use some of his friends who are subcontractors to fix up the place."

Riker had once told Trista he was a licensed general contractor, but he'd mentioned the work wasn't really his cup of tea. He really enjoyed bartending at the Liar's Club. Less stressful, he'd said. But he never said he was helping her sister with renovations.

Riker smiled while patting his tool belt. "Is the door unlocked? I'll get started now."

"Yeah, we were just leaving. Let me know what you find out?"

Riker nodded. He looked over at Trista. She felt his eyes running over her body, and a shiver went through her. Why she let him get under her skin, she didn't know. "Nice seeing you again, Riker," she said curtly and turned her attention back to Nicolette. "Let's go."

Chapter Eighteen

After lunch, Trista headed over to the theatre company for rehearsal with the kids. The play was coming along well, and she was having a lot of fun working with the children and the whole crew. It made her realize how much she missed working on Broadway. Being on television was very different. Unless you were doing live TV, it didn't matter if you messed up or forgot your lines. There were plenty of retakes. And more retakes. It could get tiring after a while. But being on Broadway was exhilarating. There was an adrenaline rush she felt every time she walked on stage to perform. The sensation of butterflies dancing in her stomach while she was in the dressing room getting ready to make her appearance. The constant questions scrolling through her mind: Would she screw up her lines? What if someone else screwed up their lines? What if she forgot her cue? Of course she never did, but there was always the possibility. The best thing of all? The thundering of applause after a great performance. The final bow after a great, kick-ass show. It couldn't be beat. Working with the children on the play was bringing back all the happy memories of her being in New York.

"The children really love working with you," Brent Glover said to her as they took a break. Brent was one of the investors of the Blue Mountain Beach Children's Theatre and came by once a week to watch rehearsals. He was an attractive man in his late thirties. Trista noticed Brent was always dressed nice in pressed khakis and a button-down shirt, no tie. Tassel loafers with no socks. Typical office attire for Florida professionals. Trista learned through their frequent chats Brent was newly single, worked as a vice president at a local private bank, and lived in a gated neighborhood in Alys Beach—the same neighborhood where Nicolette was considering moving. He was average height, dark hair with flecks of grey, and a nice smile. Trista thought he was perfect for her sister.

"These kids are amazing," Trista agreed.

"Are you thinking about sticking around for a while? You know we have the Christmas play that's always a big hit. It would be nice for you to continue working with everyone." Waiting for an answer, Brent leaned against the railing.

"I'm taking it one day at a time." Trista wasn't ready to commit to anything yet.

"Would it be forward of me to ask what you're doing tonight?" he asked.

"I was going to ask you the same thing." Trista winked, trying to put him at ease. He was obviously nervous. "How about a home-cooked meal at my place?"

Brent grinned from ear-to-ear like he had recently won the lottery. "Sure. What time?"

"Let's say seven?"

"Want me to bring anything?"

"A bottle of wine?"

"It's a date."

"I gotta get back in there." Trista exchanged phone numbers with Brent and gave him her address. "See ya tonight." She returned to the stage to finish rehearsals. She thought about what Nicolette's reaction was going to be when she brought home a blind date for her. She didn't want it to be awkward for either of them so she had to convince Nicolette that it wasn't an elaborate set-up. Trista slipped out of rehearsals a few minutes early and stopped at the local market to get the fixings for seafood paella, strawberry cheesecake, and a fresh bouquet of spring flowers.

"You're home early," Nicolette said as Trista walked in the door carrying several grocery bags.

"I'm making dinner tonight." Trista set the bags on the kitchen counter with a thud. "Seafood paella."

"Sounds yummy. Too bad I have plans."

Trista put the vegetables in the refrigerator crisper. She hadn't planned on this. Nicolette had been staying in all week. "Oh yeah? What's up?"

"Zumba at six. Then drinks with some girls at work."

"That's too bad." Trista tried to stay nonchalant as she pulled a bag of fresh strawberries out of the grocery sack. "I was making homemade cheesecake with fresh strawberry sauce. And I have a new friend coming over to eat with us."

Nicolette was checking her cell for text messages when she paused. She raised an eyebrow as she looked up at Trista. "I guess it wouldn't hurt to miss one class. Who's the new friend?"

Trista smiled triumphantly. She was counting on Nicolette's sweet tooth and curiosity to close the deal. But she continued to play it cool. "Just one of the volunteers at the theatre."

"Oh. Anyone I know?"

"I don't think so," Trista replied coyly, as started cleaning the shrimp. "Why don't you get ready? I'll make us some drinks."

"Okay," Nicolette said, eyeing her sister with suspicion. She tucked her iPhone into her pocket. "I'll grab a quick shower."

Trista smiled to herself as she started the main dish. It was one of her go-to specialties. Marla had taught her how to cook. Nicolette had no desire to learn, but Trista had loved spending time in the kitchen with their mom. By the time she had the paella simmering on the stovetop and the cheesecake in the oven, Nicolette had returned from her shower. She was dressed in a long, black maxi dress with her luxurious thick hair piled on top of her head. She wore simple gold hoops in her ears and a diamond necklace. Trista thought her sister looked beautiful, elegant and poised.

"I'm going to freshen up myself. Everything's almost ready." Trista glanced at the clock. Brent would be here within fifteen minutes.

"Do you want me to do anything?"

Trista handed her sister a margarita. On the rocks, no salt. The way she liked it. "Relax and enjoy. I'll be back in a few minutes."

She ran upstairs. After washing up, she opened her walk-in closet. There was no shortage of beautiful dresses she could wear. Tonight, however, she would be dressing down. She wanted Nicolette to be the focus of Brent's attention. She chose a simple yellow and white striped cotton dress with navy buttons halfway down the chest and on the cuffs. She had bought it during their trip to the Bahamas but never wore it. A pair of navy anchor earrings and matching necklace completed the fashionable, but casual nautical look. She slipped on a pair of Reef flip-flops and threw her hair back into an easy braid. A minimal amount of makeup—just a touch of mascara and a swipe of lip-gloss—and she was ready to go. As she was walking downstairs, she heard voices. Brent was early.

"Hello, Trista." Brent greeted her as she walked into the room. She took a look at the scene in the kitchen. Nicolette stirred the paella while Brent opened a bottle of wine.

"I see you've met my sister," Trista said, accepting a glass of white wine from him.

"Yes, I have," he replied. "If I would've known I was dining with two gorgeous women, I would've brought more wine."

Nicolette took in Trista's outfit and gave a small smirk. Trista took a hearty sip of her wine. She saw Nicolette had already taken the cheesecake out of the oven, and it was cooling on the counter. All Trista had to do was make the strawberry sauce and pop some bread in the oven.

"Why don't you take Brent out to the balcony with the appetizers, and I'll bring some more wine," Trista suggested. She took out a plate of cheese and crackers from the refrigerator and handed them to her sister. Nicolette leaned in and whispered in her ear, "I see what you're trying to do. The question is why?"

"Because I love you and want to see you happy."

"Right," Nicolette countered. She took the appetizer tray and motioned for Brent to follow her.

Trista quickly chopped the strawberries and added a teaspoon of sugar and a splash of water. After mixing the sugar water together with the fruit, she covered the bowl and put it back in the fridge. She took the seafood paella off the stovetop and put it in a decorative casserole dish, covering to keep it warm and letting the flavors meld together. She slathered a loaf of French bread with garlic butter, covered it in tin foil, and popped it in the oven for a couple of minutes. While she waited for it to warm, she sipped on her wine and peeked around the corner to see Brent and Nicolette talking on the balcony. They were both laughing. *So far so good*, she thought.

Her thoughts turned to Riker. Seeing him today was like a shock to her system. She had mistakenly thought her trip to the Bahamas would help her forget about him. After seeing him today she knew it was going to take more than a long weekend trip. She was going to have to make another call to her agent to speed up the process of getting a new job—hopefully in New York City. Far away from Blue Mountain Beach…and Riker.

Chapter Nineteen

"Dinner was great," Brent complimented her again. He wiped his mouth with a blue cloth napkin. "I love Spanish food."

"Thank you," Trista said, scooping up the last bit of cheesecake from her plate.

All through dinner, Trista tried to steer the conversation away from herself and toward Nicolette. Talking finance and real estate, which Brent and Nicolette both had in common, she thought they would make a connection. It was hard to tell if Brent was into her sister or not. He was very polite and paid equal attention to both women.

"I'll get the dishes while you two enjoy the sunset," Trista offered, picking up the dirty plates from the table.

"I can help," Brent said, getting up from his seat. He picked up his own plate and wine glass. "It's the least I can do for such a lovely meal."

"Thank you," Trista said, looking over at Nicolette. She smiled back at Trista as she refilled her wine glass.

Brent followed Trista into the kitchen. She filled the sink with hot soapy water and dumped the dishes in. "I got this. Why don't you keep Nicolette company?"

Brent put his hand on Trista's shoulder and turned her away from the sink so their eyes met. "I wanted you to know I had a really nice time tonight."

"I'm glad you took me up on my offer," Trista said.

Leaning in, he caught Trista off guard by kissing her lightly on the lips. She tried to take a step back, but she was already pushed up against the sink. Just as she was about to push Brent away, Trista heard a noise. Nicolette cleared her throat as she walked into the kitchen. Brent pulled back quickly.

"I wanted to see if I could help, but it looks like you guys have everything under control." Nicolette set her wine glass on the counter and left the room.

Trista blew out a breath. This wasn't turning out like she had hoped. *One problem at a time.* "I think you have the wrong idea, Brent."

"What do you mean?" Brent leaned against the kitchen counter, facing Trista. "I thought you invited me to dinner, to you know…get to know each other better."

Trista wiped her soapy hands on a dishtowel. "Look, I like you Brent. I'm not interested in dating anyone right now. I recently got out of a relationship and…"

"You were trying to set me up with your sister." Brent stood up straight and looked toward the balcony where Nicolette was sulking on a chaise lounge.

Trista nodded. "I'm sorry. I should've told you. I didn't mean to lead you on. You and Nicolette have a lot in common. I thought—"

He held up his hands. "Hey, it's okay. You had good intentions."

"Yeah, well…you know what they say about good intentions. Road to hell, and all that. I guess I should stick to acting. Matchmaking, apparently, is not my forte."

"Really? I think you did well. I really like your sister. She's pretty, sweet, and very smart." Brent looked toward the balcony again. "Should I go out there?"

"Not unless you want to be tossed over the balcony head first into the gulf."

"I see." Brent rocked back and forth on his heels. "Well, maybe I should shove off. I'll see you around the theatre next week. Please say goodbye to Nicolette for me."

"Sure," Trista said. "Just give it some time. Maybe call Nicolette later this week?"

Brent nodded before walking out the door.

Trista returned to the sink and rinsed the dishes before putting them inside the dishwasher. A door slammed, causing her to jump. She didn't have to turn around to know Nicolette was in the room. She could feel her sister's presence, her eyes throwing daggers at Trista's back.

"What's on your mind, Nicolette?" Trista asked, without turning around.

"What the hell was that all about?"

"I was trying to set you up with someone." Trista threw down her dishtowel and turned to face her sister. "It wouldn't hurt for you to give people a chance, Nicolette. He's a nice guy."

"Are you kidding me? I saw him trying to kiss you! He was interested in you, not me."

"I invited him to dinner for *you*. I'm not interested in him!"

"Well, obviously he wasn't interested in me." Nicolette smacked her hand on the counter. "It's always about you! You were the most popular girl in high school. Always getting what you wanted from Dad. Everything came easy for you. You even had my mom under your spell."

It wasn't lost on Trista the fact Nicolette referred to Marla as "my mom." She crossed her arms over chest, prepared for a fight. "Is this what this is about? Mom?" Trista thought she had cleared the air with Nicolette in the Bahamas. Obviously she was wrong.

"She wasn't even your mother! She felt sorry for you! Because you were the little bastard child. My dad's *big* mistake."

Trista felt like she had been stabbed in the heart. She knew Nicolette had feelings of anger against her but she never knew how deep they ran. Until now.

"Nicolette, I never asked for this. I was a little girl when Sam came out to California to find me. What was I supposed to do? Refuse to come to Florida?"

"You'll never be a part of this family! Why did you even come back here again?" Nicolette shouted.

Trista started to answer but Nicolette cut her off.

"No, wait…don't answer that. I already know. Things didn't work out for you in California, so you wanted to come back here and mess things up for me. You like seeing me miserable."

"That's not true." Trista fought back the tears welling up. "I came back to mend fences with you. Which I thought we had done last week!"

Nicolette let out a small laugh. "Yeah, you expect our problems to be fixed with one weekend in the Bahamas?" she asked, her words stabbing Trista in the heart.

Trista had reached her breaking point with her sister. She was tired of fighting the same old battle with Nicolette. "You know what, Nicolette? I've been trying to make friends with you ever since we were kids. All you've done is shove me away. You blame all your problems on me. Well, I'm sick of it. When mom got sick, I was the one taking care of her. Sam was working all the time, and you stayed away at college. *I* changed her, *I* bathed her, *I* gave her meds, and *I* held her when she couldn't stand the constant agonizing pain. She may be *your* biological mom, but she'll always be *my* mom too. And if that makes you angry, then so fucking be it!" Trista felt her face flush with anger. "I'm tired of trying to get you to like me. I. Am. Done."

"You're a real piece of work!" Nicolette grabbed her purse off the counter.

"Where are you going?" Trista asked, watching her sister pull her keys out of her purse.

"I'm not staying here another minute longer to listen to your bullshit. This is your house, not mine." Nicolette yanked the door open. "I'll be back for my things later."

Trista was shaking with fury. She felt her knees start to buckle and she let herself slide to the floor. Suddenly she was so tired. Being around Nicolette was exhausting. She curled up in a fetal position, and finally let the tears flow freely. After years of trying to get her older sister to accept her, to love her, to allow her to be a part of the family, it was over. She couldn't do this any longer.

Chapter Twenty

Trista thought she heard the door to the garage open. She figured Nicolette had come back for the rest of her stuff. Lifting her head off the kitchen floor, she saw a pair of black, dusty work boots.

"Trista? Honey, are you okay?" Riker's voice was filled with concern. He kneeled down in front of her. "What happened?"

She crawled into his arms. "Nicolette and I had a fight. It wasn't good."

"Are you hurt?" He asked, slipping his fingers through the silky stands of her hair.

Trista shook her head. "Nothing you can see on the outside."

Riker kissed her on the top of her head. "I'm sorry, baby. Your sister can be a little….a little…"

"A bitch?"

He continued to run his fingers through Trista's hair. "Want something to drink?"

She looked up at him and placed a finger on his lips. "I just want you." Their eyes locked, and Trista wondered if Riker was feeling what she felt at this very moment. A desperate need that had nothing to do with sex, but everything to do with a longing to be known, inside and out. Was there anyone in her life who truly knew who she was? Not the parts she played on television or on Broadway, but the real Trista Carmichael. She wanted Riker in her life, despite the impact it would have on her relationship with her sister. Quinn was right. It was time she started living her life for her. Not anyone else. Trista gently pressed her lips against his, relishing the softness of his lips and the intoxicating scent of his cologne.

"I've missed you," he said, giving her tiny kisses around her neck that sent electric jolts throughout her body.

"I've missed you too."

"Want to go upstairs?" He nibbled on her earlobe after whispering in her ear.

"I don't think I can wait." She needed him more than ever. "I want you, right here. Right now."

He pushed her cotton dress over her hips, planting his face firmly on her sex. Hooking a finger around the hem of her panties, he gently pulled them aside. "I'm going to make you feel so good, you'll forget about everything."

* * *

The incessant ringing of her phone pulled Trista out of a deep sleep. She rolled over and squinted at the sunlight coming through the blinds. Her cell phone was lighting up and dinging, letting her know she had a missed call and had several voicemails. She reached out for Riker, but the other side of the bed was empty. She began to wonder if last night was only a dream until she noticed a note on his pillow.

Good morning Fancy Pants,

Ran out to get breakfast. You look so beautiful sleeping I didn't want to wake you. Be back soon. Riker

Trista smiled at the note before dropping it on her nightstand. She checked her messages. The first one was from Michelle telling her that tonight's rehearsal was canceled. They would pick up rehearsals again next Thursday. The second one came from her agent with an urgent message to call her back. Trista hit the speed dial number for Kate Peterson.

"Hey, Trista," Kate greeted her as soon as she picked up the call. "Are you sitting down?"

"Yeah." Trista lay back on the pillow and waited. "What's up?"

"I've got great news! You have a special invite to casting for *Love Potion #9*."

"You're kidding me!" Trista couldn't believe her luck. She had read on the Backstage Broadway website that they were about to start casting calls for the production. The lead role—or any role for that matter—would be a dream come true. An invited call was different than an open call. Anyone can audition for an open call. But to get an invite means the casting director only wants you to audition for a certain role.

"I'm not kidding. How soon can you get here?"

Trista thought for a moment. She had to wrap up the voice-over job this morning. After that, she was free. "Tomorrow morning?"

"Great. I'll set it up with the casting director." Kate hesitated for a moment. "Are you sure you are ready for this?"

"Of course! Why?"

"Don't take this the wrong way. It's been awhile since you've done Broadway."

"I'm ready, Kate." Trista told her about the work she'd been doing with the children's theatre. "I haven't lost my touch."

"Okay then, it's settled. I'll text you the details." With a click, the phone was disconnected.

Trista heard the garage door open. She wondered what Riker had brought back for breakfast. She was hoping it was a chicken biscuit from her favorite deli. She threw on her pink, fluffy robe and took the back staircase down to the kitchen.

Trista thought about the phone call from her agent. If she hoped to make a flight out tonight, she would have to get everything together fast. She wasn't ready to tell Riker about the audition yet. Trista didn't want to jinx getting the role. She was superstitious like that and thought it would be best to keep it quiet until after she returned home.

"Good morning," Trista said cheerfully, coming around the corner to the kitchen. She stopped short when she realized Riker wasn't the one standing in her house. It was Nicolette who greeted her instead.

"Well, good morning to you." Nicolette put her briefcase down on the breakfast table.

Trista studied her sister. She was dressed for work in a conservative, navy blue dress and nude pumps. Her hair was pulled in a high ponytail. Trista recognized the outfit as one Nicolette usually reserved for big real estate closings or important client meetings. And Trista noted a big smile on her sister's face. It was a totally different Nicolette than the one who had left here last night with an ugly scowl. But Trista never knew which Nicolette she would be facing, did she? She seriously thought Nicolette had some kind of mental thing going on…bi-polar? ADHD? Her mood swings were legendary.

"Good morning," Trista said again cautiously. Where the hell was Riker? She hoped he saw Nicolette's car in the driveway before he returned.

Nicolette looked at her sister like she was out of her mind. "Mind if I have some coffee?" She grabbed a mug from the cabinet, not waiting for an answer.

"What do you want, Nic?" Trista wasn't in the mood to play games.

"I came by to say I'm sorry about yesterday." Nicolette drummed her fingernails on the counter waiting for the coffee to brew.

Trista grabbed another mug from the cabinet. She wasn't going to let her sister ruin her good mood today.

"I said some things I regret. You know, I let the ole Italian temper get the best of me. Blame it on Dad," Nicolette continued.

"You need to take responsibility for your own actions and quit blaming them on other people," Trista responded.

"Hey, I said I was sorry. I'm trying to make nice."

Trista turned to face her sister. "That's all I've been trying to do since I got in town. I wanted our relationship to work, but it takes two."

"I know that. It's why I'm here." Nicolette put a hand on hip. "Well, and also to get some of my stuff."

"Where are you going?" Trista asked. She wasn't going to ask her to stay again. She was beginning to agree it was best for Nicolette to get her own place.

"I made an offer on the townhome. It was accepted last night, and the owners want to close next week, but the renovations are going to take awhile. I'm renting the place next to the unit so I can be there every day to supervise the construction."

"Congratulations. I'm happy for you."

"How about we have dinner at my new place tonight? I can show you the plans the architect is drawing up today for the renovations." Nicolette glanced at her watch. "As a matter of fact, I'm meeting him in a few minutes."

"Thanks for the invite, but I can't tonight." Trista put her palms down on the countertop. "Listen, I have something to tell you."

"What is it?"

"I have a meeting in New York tomorrow. My agent called me this morning and wants me to get on the first flight out."

Nicolette sipped on her coffee. "Is this an audition for another TV series?"

"No, it's not." Trista wasn't ready to share the details with her sister either.

"All right. Well, when are you leaving?"

"Tonight. I'll be back in a couple of days. So, it's no rush for you to leave."

Nicolette smiled. "Does this mean you'll be moving soon?"

Trista didn't know if her sister was smiling because Trista may be moving to New York or if she was genuinely happy for her. With Nicolette, it was hard to tell. "I have some things in the works, so yeah, I might. One step at a time though."

Nicolette came around the kitchen counter and hugged her sister. "Well, good luck. Whatever it is you having going on, I'm sure you'll be happy!"

"Thanks."

"I'll be back after my meeting to pack." Nicolette started to leave when something caught her attention. Trista followed her sister's gaze to the breakfast table where an Atlanta Braves baseball cap sat. Her whole body tensed up.

"Is that James's hat?" Nicolette asked, walking over to it and picking it up.

Oh crap. Trista tried to come up with something fast. Riker must have taken it off when he came into the kitchen last night. "Is that his hat? I found it in the house when I was cleaning up the other day. I meant to ask you about it."

"Huh," Nicolette said. "He must've left it over here after his birthday party. I'll return it to him."

"Okay," Trista said, relieved she had dodged a bullet. She breathed a heavy sigh of relief when Nicolette left. She would have to remember to tell him about it so they could keep their story straight. *Fuck.* Trista hoped Nicolette didn't get a chance to talk to Riker before she did.

After the morning melee, she had a big headache brewing. Opening her kitchen's junk drawer, Trista plucked out a packet of Goody's. She opened her mouth and poured the bitter powder down her throat, chasing it with a gulp of coffee. "That's what you get for lying to your sister *and* your boyfriend," she said out loud.

Chapter Twenty-One

The limo driver expertly weaved in and out of traffic. The hundreds of skyscrapers beleaguered the city blocking the sun. Trista didn't think she would ever get used to the dizziness she always experienced when riding through the crowded New York City streets. She cracked open the window to get some fresh air, trying not to get sick.

The driver caught her attention in the rearview mirror and stated, "We're almost there," in his thick Brooklyn accent.

Trista nodded. She had forgotten about the distinct smell of the city. After living at the beach—without the LA smog—with nice, clean air and a salty sea breeze, she thought maybe she was sensitive to overpowering smells. And depending on the area of the city, it could smell like hot dogs and fresh-baked bagels, or in this case, a garbage-y sewer smell. Rolling up the window, she decided to take her chances on the limo's pine-scented air freshener.

Trista had lived in Florida long enough to have permanent saltwater in her veins. But she also loved the city. She thrived on it. The energy. The people. The flow. New York was a place where dreams were made. This is where she got her start in show business. "I used to live here," Trista replied to the driver's inquiry as to whether she was visiting for pleasure or business. "I hope to move back soon."

The driver pulled over at the curb, and she exited the limo, instructing him to wait for her—she wouldn't be long. Taking the elevator up to the forty-sixth floor, she walked into the offices of the PETERSON AGENCY. The reception area was dark except for a lone lamp emitting a soft glow on the desk. It was after eight o'clock at night.

"Kate?" she called out.

"Back here!"

Trista walked down the narrow corridor toward a corner office at the end.

"Well, hello there," Kate greeted her. "How was your flight?"

"Long."

"I'm glad you could make it." Kate stood from her desk, and they exchanged quick air kisses on each cheek.

Kate was in her late fifties, but she didn't look a day over forty. She had shiny, brunette hair that hung stylishly at her collarbone, and she wore her trademark, blood-red lipstick on her artificially plump lips. Trista thought Kate had a certain look—a driven, take-no-bullshit look—that most born-and-bred New Yorkers had. Although, she knew Kate had a soft side too, once you got to really know her. Kate had been Trista's first agent, before Trista moved to Hollywood. She'd helped Trista maneuver through the New York City lifestyle and the ins-and-outs of the acting business.

"Here it is." Kate slid a sheaf of papers across her desk. "Your audition time was moved to ten thirty. Is it all right?"

Crap. She thought she had more time to memorize her lines and prepare for the audition. "I'll make it work."

Kate smiled. "You'll do fine."

Trista looked over the first page. The fluttery feeling was back in her stomach. She really wanted this. It was what she needed to kick off her career again. And get away from all the drama with her sister.

"Thanks for the vote of confidence."

"Not to bring up bad news, Trista, but did you hear about Blake?"

Trista paused. "Um, no."

"I didn't think so." Kate picked up her electronic cigarette and inhaled. She blew smoke through her nose. "He's getting married."

Trista snorted. "Who would want to marry that piece of shit?"

"Melanie Sweetwater."

Trista laughed. "Really? She's a washed-up drunk who got fired from *Days of Our Lives*. Good riddance."

"You haven't been keeping up with the news, have you?" Katie blew a ring of smoke. It faintly smelled like cherries. "Melanie is the new lead on *You Only Live Once*."

"What?" Trista scooted up to the edge of her seat. "You have to be fucking kidding me! She took my place? When did this happen? I thought they weren't going to replace my role."

"She's playing the role of your cousin. You really didn't know?"

"Let me guess. Blake's her agent?"

"Yep."

Trista gripped the papers. She flashed back to the picture of Blake and Melanie on the magazine cover. It really was a serious relationship. Why hadn't Quinn called her to give her this news? Then again, why did she care? She left that world behind months ago. She had an opportunity to do something she loved again. "Well, good for them." She stood up to go, putting a smile back on her face. "I have to go back to the hotel and get busy."

"That's my girl. Don't let all the other stuff bother you."

"Thanks again, Kate."

Blowing another round of smoke, Kate nodded. "Call me afterwards. Let me know how it goes."

***

Trista picked up a room key from the front desk and made her way to the hotel room. Feeling ravenous, she decided to order a steak from room service and watched a few minutes of some silly housewives reality show. Trista eyed the script she had tossed on the bed and then kicked off her shoes. While she was waiting for room service, she decided to take a quick shower and put on her PJs. The rest of the night would be devoted to learning her lines and getting into character.

After her shower, Trista wrapped herself up in the luxurious hotel robe. She picked up the script and stretched out across the bed. The script highlighted her character as ANNA PENNINGTON. The lead female role of *Love Potion #9*. If she got this role, it would mean at least a twelve-month run on Broadway if reviews went well. Trista would be willing to sign a year contract if she had to. Afterwards, she could decide whether to return to TV or maybe even consider the possibility of a movie role. Of course, she had to get the role first.

Her cell phone rang, and she checked the caller ID. Riker. "Hello?"

"Hey there. I was calling to see if everything was going okay."

Earlier that morning, after Nicolette had left, Riker had shown up with bagels and donuts. He had explained to Trista he had seen Nicolette's car in the driveway and had circled around the block a few times waiting for her to leave. Trista told him what happened with her sister and that they had temporarily called a truce. She didn't tell him, however, she was going to New York to audition for a role on Broadway. Instead she told him she was going to be spending some long days in the studio finishing up some voice-over work. Superstitious, Trista didn't want to jeopardize getting the lead role on Broadway she desperately wanted by telling anyone she was in town.

"I miss you," Trista answered.

"I miss you, too," Riker said, before covering the handset and yelling at someone. "Sorry, babe, but it's crazy at the bar tonight. I wanted to see how work was going. I'll call you in the morning, okay?"

"Sure, good night." Trista disconnected the call and then turned off her phone. She didn't need any distractions. Turning her attention back to the script, Trista read her lines over and over, memorizing each one.

***

The same limo driver picked up Trista and dropped her off at the theatre where the auditions were being held. She had expected a waiting room full of people, but she was the only person there.

An assistant greeted her at the door. "The casting director will be with you shortly."

She tried to settle her nerves while she waited. She wondered how many other people they were considering for the part. Kate had said she didn't know.

Her cell phone vibrated in her purse. She quickly checked the screen. It was Riker calling. She let it go to voicemail and turned off her phone to prevent further distractions. The last thing she needed was Riker in her head. She ran through her lines again.

The assistant was back minutes later. "Miss Carmichael? Tom Elder will see you now." She led Trista to an empty room. Two chairs sat facing a wall. "Have a seat. He'll be right in."

A minute later a very tall gentlemen walked in. He was thin with wispy, grey hair and wire spectacles. They shook hands. The assistant closed the door behind her.

“Is there anyone else joining us?” Trista asked.

“Nope. Just me.”

Trista looked around uncomfortably for a second. This was not the norm. Usually there was at least a few casting members in the audience. Sometimes even the producer.

“Is there something wrong?” Tom asked.

“No. I thought someone would read with me.”

“I will,” he replied. He had a sheet of paper in his hands, but he didn’t look at it. “I’m ready when you are.”

Trista took a few deep breaths to calm herself. She tried not to let the situation control her. She closed her eyes and slipped into character. And then she uttered the first line in the play.

“Do you believe in love at first sight?”

Chapter Twenty-Two

Kate didn't even wait for Trista to say hello when she picked up the phone. "It must've gone well because they've already asked you for a callback."

"Really?" Trista wasn't sure she had done all that well at the audition. She flubbed a few lines, but in the end she got through it. She told Kate about being the only person in the room with Tom during the audition.

Kate laughed. "I should've warned you about Tom. He doesn't like anyone in the room when the leading character reads for a part for the first time. Says it messes with his synergy or something. Anyway, honey, he wants to see you again. This time, you will probably read with the other casting director, and there may be other people in the room." Kate lowered her voice. "I hear they have another girl reading for the part. So don't be surprised if she's there too."

"Who?" Trista asked.

"Leigha Epler."

"I thought she was in drug rehab for heroin or something. Didn't she get fired from another play?"

"She was released from rehab early. Tom wants her to read for this. I wouldn't worry too much about it. I wanted you to know what you were walking into."

"All right. What time?"

"Can you be there in an hour?"

Trista didn't have anything else important to do. She had planned on playing tourist today and maybe taking a tour of the Statue of Liberty, eat a hotdog at Gray's Papaya, and stroll around Times Square while she waited to hear back about the play. "Of course."

***

This time Trista was met by Tom Elder himself. He escorted her back to the same room and introduced her to Brandy Thibault, the other casting director, and David Browman, who had already been cast as the male lead in the play.

"I have to say I was surprised to hear I was going to be reading with the beautiful Trista Carmichael. I thought you were still doing television," David said. She wasn't sure if it was a dig or if he was being nice. She took it as the former.

"You know I started on Broadway. I was Ali in *Rent* back in 2005."

The door clicked shut. "It was a small part, a long time ago. You had what? Three lines in the whole play?" a woman's voice asked.

Trista turned to find Leigha Epler entering the room.

"Leigha! How are you?" Trista asked, forcing a tight smile on her face.

Leigha was well known around Broadway, having several plum roles, before her brief stint in rehab. But Trista wasn't going to stoop to her level and bring it up.

Leigha tossed her trademark blonde mane over her shoulders. “I’m doing terrific!” She was gorgeous, thin, and had a voice Broadway producers loved. The voice of an angel, some people thought. Trista heard Leigha’s mother had spent a fortune on voice lessons, acting coaches, and who knows what else when Leigha was growing up. And Leigha graduated from one of the best performing arts schools in New York. Trista had a right to be worried about this role.

Trista felt her stomach tightened. She put on a fake smile. “Nice seeing you again.”

Leigha sat down on one of the chairs and crossed her long legs at the ankle. “Always good to see you, dear.”

“Okay, girls. Let’s get started.” Tom took his seat. “Trista, why don’t you read first?” He thrust a sheaf of papers at her. “This is the new script. We made some changes.”

A cold read. Trista looked over the script. A cold read was exactly that—an actor/actress was to read a part he/she had never seen before. She didn’t have time to prepare. But she knew the character. She could do this. Taking a deep breath to mentally prepare, she read the lines.

Chapter Twenty-Three

Trista let the top down on her Mercedes and felt the warmth of the fresh Florida sunshine as it hit her face. It felt good to be back in Florida, but she was already missing the vibe of the city. She decided to drive straight to Riker's place. He had sent her a text earlier asking her to stop by if she had time. She had been putting him off while she was in New York, explaining she was busy with work.

Trista parked her Mercedes in the driveway and turned off the ignition. Reaching into her bag, she pulled out some mint flavored Chapstick and applied it to her lips. Riding in a plane always made her skin and lips dry, and she didn't have a lot of time to freshen up in the airplane's lavatory. Squeezing into a little box of a bathroom to change clothes and apply makeup on an airplane experiencing slight turbulence wasn't the most ideal situation. She spritzed some of her favorite perfume, Flowerbomb, on her neck and wrists and then got out of the car.

Before she could knock, the front door swung open. Riker was standing there, shirtless, with a goofy smile on his face. He was horny. Trista could tell. She was too.

Riker grabbed Trista by the hand and pulled her inside his apartment without saying a word. As soon as the door was closed and bolted, he picked her up and carried her to his bedroom. Gently laying her across the bed, he straddled her and leaned over, covering her mouth with his. His tongue tangled with hers as she ran her hands over his body, feeling the muscular bulge of his biceps, the hardness of his chest, and each ripple of his abs. Riker pulled back and started to unbutton her shirt. He lifted her bra, freeing her breasts from their black, lacy cups. Putting his mouth over one nipple, he gave it a hard tug. Trista moaned in pleasure.

Riker moved on to the other breast and licked her nipple, swirling his tongue around. She could feel his hardness against her thigh. With one hand, he pushed up her skirt, finding Trista wasn't wearing any underwear.

"Oh my God, you're so hot right now."

Trista arched her back as Riker settled between her legs. He ran his tongue over her swollen clit. "You taste so sweet." He pulled her clit into his mouth and sucked, causing her to slip into complete ecstasy. When she thought she couldn't take anymore, he slipped his finger deep inside while tasting every inch of her, sending her world into an explosion of vibrant colors.

"I've missed you so much," Riker said as he stripped off his jeans in record time and lowered himself back over her. She could feel the tip of his shaft penetrate her as he pushed up against her. Trista opened her legs even more as Riker slipped easily inside. She cried out in ecstasy as he plunged deeper.

Grabbing a handful of his hair, she held on as he continued to pump with long, steady strokes. He threw his head back, letting out a groan as he began to pick up the pace, moving faster and faster. She picked up her hips and ground against him, meeting his every thrust.

"You're so fucking incredible. I love the way you feel, Trista," Riker said as he moved inside of her.

"I have missed this," Trista answered breathlessly. "I can't get enough."

Riker slowed his rhythm, easing in and out with nice long strokes while rubbing her swollen clit with his thumb. "How does that feel?" he asked.

"I can't hold back any longer," she answered, as a crashing wave of pleasure swept over her. She cried out his name as she came.

He growled as he plunged inside of her one last time, collapsing gently on top of her.

"I've missed you," she whispered in his ear. She played with his hair twisting the soft brown tendrils around her finger.

"You have no idea how much I've missed you," he finally said, catching his breath. He kissed her on the neck before easing out. He rolled over and tucked his arms behind his head on the pillow. "Are you done with work?"

Trista nodded, swallowing her guilty conscience. "For now. I'm hoping to get some more projects."

"Sounds like a perfect time for a little vacation."

"Oh yeah? Where did you have in mind?"

"Key West."

Trista scooched over, and nuzzled her head against Riker's arm. "What's in the Keys?"

"The Bar."

Trista laughed. "What bar?"

"Not just any bar. The Bar. That's the name of it."

"You want to go all the way to the Keys to visit a bar? We have plenty of them here in Blue Mountain."

"My friend, Stan Hayes, owns The Bar. He called me last night and asked me if I wanted to buy it. He recently got married and is moving back to Panama City Beach."

Trista lifted her head and stared at Riker. "You're serious?"

"Cross my heart." He made the motion with his fingers over his chest. "I've always loved the Keys. And it's a great opportunity. He's selling it dirt cheap."

"Maybe there's something wrong with it?"

"I doubt it. The Bar is the most popular hangout in the area." Riker kissed her on top of her nose. "So what do you say? Want to go check it out with me?"

"Wait a minute. You're serious. You want to buy a bar in the Keys? Like, move down there permanently?"

He nodded. "I'd love for you to come with me."

"Riker. I don't know if I can do it." She thought about the job in New York. Long distance relationships almost never worked. "I have my career to think about."

"Miami isn't far away. I've been doing some research. They do a lot of filming around there. There's a ton of studios for your voice-over work. Plus with the international airport, you can pretty much fly anywhere you need to be at a moment's notice. Don't a lot of actors have houses around Miami?"

Trista nodded and closed her eyes to think about everything for a moment. It kind of irked her that he had been planning this for a while and never mentioned it to her. Then again she never said anything to him about her plans for Broadway either. And she knew this was as good a time as any to tell him about New York. He didn't understand the way her business worked. She couldn't up and move to Miami or the Keys. She had to go where the work was, and right now, there was nothing in South Florida that appealed to her.

On the other hand, she was falling in love with Riker and it scared her. It scared her a lot. Her last relationship hadn't ended so well. Not that she thought Riker was anything like Blake. Plus, she still had to deal with the emotional fall-out from Nicolette once she learned of her and Riker's relationship. No, now was not the time to deal with all this. She hadn't heard anything back from her agent, anyway. She shook all the thoughts from her head.

Riker took her chin in his hand and gently turned her to face him. "What's wrong, Fancy Pants? I can see those wheels turning in that pretty little head of yours."

She put on a smile. "Since when can you see inside of my head?" she teased him. Trista wanted to be supportive of Riker and his dreams, too. What would a quick trip to the Keys hurt? She could use a romantic get-away. "When do you want to go?"

"We can fly down there after rehearsals on Saturday. Come back Monday or Tuesday night. I already have Big Dave covering my shifts at the Liar's Club."

Trista thought about getting the call regarding the job on Broadway. When she left New York, they still hadn't made a final decision on casting. Kate had told her it might take a few days before they heard anything. As far as she knew, they could be looking at other actresses. What if she had to leave again at a moment's notice? She could always call her agent and let her know she was going on a quick trip. Worst-case scenario, she could make an excuse to fly home early and catch a flight from Miami.

"It'll be fun." Riker pulled Trista closer to him. "Besides we can have some alone time without worrying about Nicolette or anyone else seeing us. I know of this little private island down there we can stay at a night or two. It's totally secluded. Adults only."

Trista couldn't say no to Riker. Getting away from Blue Mountain Beach and the drama with her sister would be refreshing. Besides it would give her the perfect chance to tell him about her plans for moving to New York. Whether she got the job or not, she thought the move would be the best thing for her if she still wanted a career in acting. If he loved her, they could make it work.

Trista stretched out. "Are you going to help me pack?"

Riker replied, "Just throw a couple bikinis in your bag. And a toothbrush. That's all you need." He glanced at the clock on the nightstand. "We need to get going if we are going to make rehearsals tonight."

Chapter Twenty-Four

After rehearsal was over, Trista drove home. When she pulled up to the house, she saw a familiar car in the driveway. An old, dark-green Ford F-150 pickup truck that needed a good wash and detail job. She smiled to herself. What a surprise to come home to. The front door was unlocked, and she let herself inside.

"Trista? Is that you?"

A plump gentleman with thick grey hair and an olive complexion came walking toward her.

"Dad! What a surprise!" Trista gave her father a hug. "I thought you were gone until the end of the month."

"When I heard my little girl had moved back home, I decided to cut my trip short." He returned her hug and gave her a kiss on the cheek. "It is so good to see you."

"You too, Dad."

"Where's your sister? I've been trying to call her all day."

"She didn't tell you?"

"Tell me what?"

"She moved out."

"What? When?"

"A few days ago. She's buying a new house."

"I knew that. But I thought she was doing renovations first."

"Well…" Trista shrugged.

"You two had another falling out?"

She pushed her index finger and thumb close together. "A little one."

"All I ever wanted was for you girls to get along…"

"Sam?" A woman's voice called out. "Where are you?"

Trista looked around, startled. "Who's that?"

"Madeline! I'm in the living room. Come here and meet Trista."

"Dad?" Trista asked again.

"A very nice lady who I met while on vacation in Greece."

"She came home with you?" Trista whispered.

Madeline came into view. She was an attractive lady in her late sixties with rich auburn hair and hazel eyes. The first thing Trista noticed about Madeline was her hot-pink lipstick, which matched her hot-pink pantsuit and shoes. Instead of clashing with her reddish-blonde hair, she somehow made it work. Lots of gold bangles jingled on both of her arms when she hugged Trista.

"Your dad has told me so much about you and your sister…I feel like I already know you."

"I wish I could say the same about you," Trista said, laughing.

Her dad shot her a warning look. "Words cannot describe this beautiful lady, Trista. I thought you girls should meet her in person."

An awkward silence ensued for a moment. Trista stared between Madeline and her father. Even though she hadn't seen her father in a while, it was not like him to bring home a woman he had recently met. However, it was his life—who was she to interfere? She had enough problems going on without adding her dad and his new fling to it.

Her father cleared his throat. "I thought we could all have dinner together."

It was then Trista noted the smell of garlic and tomatoes wafting through the house.

"I hope you haven't eaten yet," her father said.

"No, actually I'm starving."

"I'm calling your sister again. I want her to come meet Madeline as well."

Good luck with that. She wondered if Nicolette had come by and cleaned out her closet yet. She watched as her father dialed the number.

"Why don't we go have a glass of wine? Sit outside on the deck and talk?" Madeline suggested.

Something about Madeline rubbed Trista the wrong way. This was her house. Shouldn't she be offering Madeline a glass of wine? It was like she just stepped into a Twilight Zone episode. "Okay," Trista answered. "I'm going to freshen up. I'll meet you outside."

As she ran up the stairs, she heard her father talking to Nicolette. Arguing with her was more like it. She didn't need to hear the outcome of the conversation. She knew her dad would give Nicolette no choice but to come over and eat dinner. Nicolette couldn't say no to her father any more than Trista could.

Trista stopped on the second floor and peeked into Nicolette's room. Everything looked the same. She opened the closet door. It was empty. So she had officially moved out.

What would Nicolette's reaction be when she told her about Riker? Now that she wasn't living here, it was probably as good a time as any to tell her. There was also a good possibility they would never speak again after having this conversation. Was it a chance she was willing to take?

"Everything okay?" A voice behind her startled Trista. She turned to find her father standing in the doorway.

Trista quickly shut the closet door. "Um, yeah. Everything is fine."

"Are you doing okay?"

Trista shook her head. Tears welled up in her eyes. Her father walked over and gave her a hug.

"I know things haven't been easy on you, baby girl." He continued to hold her in his arms. "I don't have to tell you it's going to take some time with Nicolette." He pulled back and took her face in his hands. "Do you want to talk about it?"

"Not really."

"Why don't you go freshen up? Have a glass of wine with Madeline while I get dinner on the table. We'll talk about everything in the morning."

"Okay." She looked up at her father as he planted a kiss on her forehead.

***

Trista was getting to know Madeline. They were working on their third glass of wine when she heard voices coming from inside.

"It sounds like your sister is here," Madeline said.

They both stood up from the couch. Trista took one last view of the gulf. The waves were growing as storm clouds threatened the horizon. Angry black clouds were gathering with quickening speed. The wind was picking up and blew the unlatched screen door shut with a loud thud. Trista secured the latch as they walked by.

"Even with the storm approaching, the gulf is still beautiful. There's something about its quiet strength and determination to thrive under all kinds of conditions. Have you ever noticed how gorgeous the beach is after a tropical storm? There's a kind of peace and serenity," Madeline observed.

Trista took one last look at the beach and nodded. She thought the metaphor was perfect for the situation between her and Nicolette. "Let's take this inside. Smells like dinner's ready." Hearing Nicolette's voice, she wondered what kind of mood her sister was in tonight.

When Trista arrived inside, she found another surprise guest in the living room with her father. *What the hell is going on?* Riker was standing next to Nicolette.

"We have another guest for dinner," her father said. "Trista, have you meet Nicolette's boyfriend yet?"

Trista stopped dead in her tracks. Why was Riker here with her sister? After rehearsal was over, he said he was going home to pack for their trip. His last words were, "See ya in the morning, babe." So what the hell was he doing in her kitchen? With her sister?

Nicolette pulled Riker closer to her. "Dad, they've met before. Remember I told you about James's surprise birthday party? The night Trista arrived in town?"

"Right. I forgot. Your old man is…well, getting old. Well, Madeline hasn't met him yet."

Trista watched as Madeline's eyes lit up. She was staring Riker up and down like he was going to be the main course tonight.

"Nice to meet you, James." She glanced at Nicolette. "What a catch, dear."

Trista could feel her blood boiling. Her sister didn't even try to explain Riker wasn't her boyfriend anymore. And Riker didn't even bother to correct her. It also grated her nerves Nicolette called Riker by his first name. It sounded so formal…not at all like the person he was. Nicolette gave Trista a smirkish grin. *Just what the fuck was happening here?* She waited for Riker to say something. Anything. He definitely looked uncomfortable.

"Well, let's eat." Her dad pointed to the spread on the dining room table. It was covered with all kinds of delectable Italian dishes. Spaghetti and meatballs, lasagna, Italian pork sausages, garlic bread, and salad. Normally a nice home-cooked meal like this would whet Trista's appetite. Her dad was known for his legendary Italian dishes. But instead her stomach was tied in knots. She felt sick. All the wine she had drunk was going straight to her head—muddling her thoughts and fueling her desire to beat the shit out of her sister and give Riker a good ass-kicking as well.

"I haven't had a chance to talk to you in a while, Daddy. I have some good news!"

"You're getting married!" Madeline blurted out.

Apparently she had too much wine as well. Trista looked over at Riker. His face was turning all kinds of red.

Her father set down his wine glass.

Nicolette laughed. *She is thoroughly enjoying this.* Trista had to wonder what if Nicolette had any idea about her and Riker. She was enjoying this moment a little too much. Something was definitely brewing in that sinister head of hers.

"Not yet," Nicolette finally said. "I bought the townhouse down the road; I told you about it. We closed yesterday."

"Well, congratulations." Her dad raised his wine glass. "Salute."

Everyone clinked their glasses together. Trista continued to look at Riker. To get any kind of clue to what the fuck was going on. He only gave her a quick smile.

"I've rented the unit next door so I can oversee renovations. James has been helping me get all the contractors together to start the work."

"Is that what you do? Build houses?" Madeline asked, eyeing his muscular arms. "I bet you get quite a workout."

Riker choked on his wine before recovering. He wiped his lips with a cloth napkin. "I'm a bartender by trade. I have my Florida contractor's license, but I only do odd jobs here and there."

"Don't be so modest, honey." Nicolette leaned into Riker. She turned her attention to Madeline and her father. "He could run his own business if he wanted to. Instead he likes working at the bar."

Riker shrugged. "It's a stress-free job." He looked at Trista; she could tell he was trying to get her attention, but she looked away.

Her father must have noticed the awkwardness between the three of them. "Trista, try some of my lasagna. It's meat free."

"Meat free!" Nicolette said loudly. "What's up with that? You've never made anything meat free in your life."

"The doctor said he has to start watching his cholesterol and high blood pressure," Madeline interrupted. "I've been trying to get him to start eating more vegetables and fruits."

Trista watched as her dad loaded her plate with spinach lasagna. The dish was loaded with cheese. *Not sure how that's going to help matters*. She looked around the table. Had she been living a dream the last couple of months? Because it sure felt like it. Who were these people? Her dad showed up with a lady he recently met—a lady who acted like she was already part of the family. Then her sister showed up with Riker, and acting like they were still a couple. Meanwhile, she had just had sex with Riker not more than a few hours ago. She had agreed to go to Key West with him. *What the fuck was going on?* She couldn't take this anymore. Trista stood and picked up her plate. "I'm not feeling well. Please excuse me."

Her dad put his hand on her arm. "Are you okay?"

"Yeah, Dad. I'll be fine."

As she started to walk toward the kitchen, she heard Nicolette launch into a story about meeting with a plumber with the "worst case of plumber's crack" she'd ever seen. Madeline's throaty laugh filled the room.

Trista dumped the contents of her plate into the trash and started to rinse the plate in the sink. She felt a pair of hands on shoulders. She tensed up.

"I'm sorry, babe. I know this is weird and awkward, but it's not what it seems," Riker whispered in her ear.

Trista whirled around. "Then please tell me what the fuck *is* happening here? Because it seems you and my sister have a thing going on!"

"Shhhh…" Riker tried to put his finger over her mouth, but she pushed him away.

"I'm tired of all the lies and secrecy, Riker."

"If I remember correctly, I'm the one who wanted to tell your sister about us. You're the one who wanted to wait! Let's tell her right now."

"Now is not the time," Trista said. "Not with my dad and his lady friend here. Besides, it seems Nicolette is already planning your wedding…to her!"

He laughed. "I'm not marrying your sister. I'm in love with you. You know that."

"No, I don't know that," she said, still holding the plate in her hands. He took it from her and put in the sink. "I love you, Trista Carmichael. Will you please let me explain what happened tonight?"

"This is not how I imagined it would be when you first told me you loved me."

"It is what it is. I love you, and I want to tell everyone."

"So what happened?" Trista leaned against the counter and folded her arms across her chest.

"After rehearsals, I went home. Nicolette was waiting for me inside."

"She has a key to your place?"

"I guess I forgot to get my key from her when we broke up." Riker shrugged. "Anyway, she asked me to go out to dinner with her. To discuss the plans for renovations on her new townhome. I tried to tell her *no*, but you know how persistent your sister is. I told her I would go to dinner with her, but this was going to be it. After tonight, she was on her own with the renovations." He put his arms around Trista. "I promise you, that's it. I didn't realize her idea of dinner tonight would be coming to your house and meeting your father. Apparently, your father called Nic at the last minute and asked her to come to here. This has been a little awkward for me too. How am I supposed to explain to your father I'm not dating Nicolette but, in fact, in love with his other daughter?"

Trista knew he was right. Tonight wasn't the place or the time, but they need to rectify the situation with Nicolette very soon.

Riker caressed her cheek. "I thought we could talk about sitting down with Nicolette together and telling her about us when we got back from the Keys. It's time for us to move on with our lives. I'm tired of hiding my feelings for you."

Trista pursed her lips together in thought. "What about Madeline? She's been staring at you like you're the main course."

He laughed. "As far as your dad's lady friend, I'm sure she's harmless. She's obviously head over heels for your father."

She stood on her tiptoes and kissed him, feeling the tension leave her body as Riker caressed her back. She forgot all about Nicolette and her father and his lady friend. Everything was blissful for about twenty seconds…until she heard Sam clear his throat.

Trista immediately pushed Riker away. Her dad was standing by the kitchen counter with an empty wine bottle in his hands.

"Excuse me. I was getting another bottle of vino for the table."

"Uh, Dad—" Trista started.

"Mr. Carmichael—" Riker said at the same time.

"It's really complicated," Trista started to explain.

Sam waved them off. "It's really none of my business." He opened the wine cooler and selected another bottle of red. "I've got a couple nice Cuban cigars if you'd like to join me on the balcony, son."

Riker looked at Trista with a hint of fear in his eyes.

"Go ahead." She pulled a glass from the cabinet and filled it with water. "I'm going to take some aspirin and lie down for a bit."

Trista watched as her father and Riker left the room. Riker turned and looked at her one last time. He mouthed, "I love you."

She blew him a kiss. *Riker is right. We need to tell Nicolette as soon as we get back from the Keys.*

Chapter Twenty-Five

The next morning Trista found her father in the kitchen holding a coffee mug. He had the newspaper spread across the breakfast table. "Good morning," she greeted him. "Would you like some more coffee?"

Sam raised his mug. "This is green tea. Another life change the doctor insisted I make. No more caffeine."

Trista looked concerned as she filled the reservoir with filtered water. "What have you done with my father?"

"Hey, I'm not getting any younger. I need to watch my diet if I'm ever going to live to see you and your sister get married. And give me some grandbabies. Speaking of…" he said, eyeing her warily.

"Where's Madeline?" Trista asked, cutting him off. She wasn't ready to discuss Riker, at least not without some caffeine running through her veins.

"She's taking a walk on the beach. I told her I would make us some breakfast when she got back."

"She seems like a really nice lady," Trista commented as she inserted a pod of Jet Fuel in the Keurig. Turning the brew switch to ON, she patiently waited.

"She is a nice lady." Her dad put down the paper and played with the teabag in his cup. "I know this seems sudden, honey. But I really like Madeline. After my health scare—"

"What health scare?"

"Now, it's no big deal. I had a minor heart attack."

"What? When? Why didn't you tell me?"

"Like I said, it was no big deal. I'd been having some chest discomfort and pain in my left hand. Madeline and I were having dinner on the cruise, and I started feeling sick. She took me to the ship's doctor, and he ran an EKG. Said he thought I'd had a heart attack. They immediately airlifted me to the hospital in Greece. I only stayed a couple of days. The cardiologist said it was a myocardial infarction. They inserted a stent. The doctor told me I needed to change my lifestyle, eating habits…well, you know."

"I can't believe I'm finding out about this now. Does Nicolette know?"

"I told her last night. Like I said—"

"I know Dad. It's no big deal." Trista sighed. She realized the coffee was done. She generously added a splash of cream. "Well, it's a big deal to me."

"I'm fine, really. Madeline has been taking really good care of me."

"Where did you two meet?"

"I met her the first night of the cruise. We've been together since."

Her father had left Florida three months ago to take a cruise around the world. His best friend from college, Larry, had talked him into going together. Larry was a widower, too. He had heard cruises were the best way to meet women their age. So they booked themselves on a senior citizens' European cruise, and visited such exotic ports as

Greece, Turkey, France, and Italy. Sam had been reluctant at first, but when he heard there was gambling on cruise ships he agreed to go.

"I plan on asking her to marry me."

"What? Dad, you can't be serious. You've only known each other for three months!"

"At my age, three months is equal to three years. It's not easy meeting women my age."

"Are you kidding me? Florida is crawling with older divorcees, Dad."

"Gold diggers, honey. I've been through enough of them to know. They're all after your money. Madeline is close to my age. And she has her own money."

Trista blew on her coffee before taking a sip. Her dad was right. There were plenty of gold diggers in the area. She had heard about them firsthand from Riker. Riker's father had been taken to the cleaners by his last wife. She was twenty-five years younger and on her third marriage. Riker's father said she had never walked away from a marriage with anything less than a half million dollars settlement. "Where's Madeline from?"

"St. Petersburg, Florida."

"So you'll live here?"

"Actually we were thinking about settling down in Boca."

"Boca Raton?"

"The retirement capital of Florida."

"What about all the business you have here?"

"Your sister can handle it. It's time I handed the reins over to her anyway." Her dad peered at her. "Unless you want a piece of it?"

"I don't know the first thing about real estate investments, Dad." Trista sipped her coffee. She didn't have the greatest track record with realtors either. “I do think it’s a great idea, though. Nicolette would be the best choice. With your heart attack, early retirement sounds like a good idea.”

Her dad patted the seat next to him. “Now, tell me about what’s going on with you and James.”

“It’s Riker, Dad.”

“Huh?” her dad asked, confused.

“He likes to go by his last name. Riker. And it’s a long story.”

“We have time.”

Trista sighed. “I met Riker the first night I came back home. I had stopped at the Liar’s Club for a drink. He wasn’t dating Nicolette at the time. As a matter of fact, they had been broken up for several weeks. But you know how Nicolette is.”

“She doesn’t give up easy,” Sam said with a nod. “She’s a chip off the old block, as they say.”

“That’s putting it mildly.” Trista pushed some newspaper out of the way.

“Let me guess. Nicolette doesn’t know about you two.”

“We’ve been waiting for a good time to tell her.” Trista told her dad about her plans to go to the Keys with Riker.

“Take it from me, honey. There’s never a good time when dealing with your sister. Just do it, get it over with. She’ll be okay.”

Trista said, “It’s been over twenty years since I came from California to live you. She’s still not over it.”

He reached over and grabbed her hand, giving it a squeeze. “Your sister loves you very much. Yes, she can be a little difficult and act like she doesn’t care about you. But I know otherwise.”

“What are you talking about?”

Sam shifted in his seat. "When you were about seven years old you came down with the chicken pox."

Trista nodded. "I remember. Itching from head to toe."

"Those scratches caused a bad infection. You were in the hospital for about ten days fighting it." He cleared his throat. "We were all worried sick about you. Especially Nicolette. One night I went to tuck her in, and I found your sister kneeling bedside praying out loud for you. Tears were streaming down her cheeks. She asked me if you were going to die."

"Dad, that's very sweet. But it was a long time ago."

"She cares for you, Trista. She always has."

"She has a crappy way of showing it."

"When you left for New York, Nicolette was in a funk for months. Unfortunately, she's a lot like me. She holds a lot inside. She may not show it, but she does care for you. She loves you."

"She's not going to care for me when I tell her about Riker."

Her dad got up and started to fold the newspapers. He paused and patted Trista on the back. "Everything is going to be okay."

The sliding glass door from the balcony opened, and Madeline walked in holding a large, red bucket. A smile beamed across her face. "Lookie what I got this morning. I can't believe all the shells and sand dollars I found on my walk."

"Good morning, Madeline. Would you like some coffee?" Trista offered.

"No thank you, dear. I had some tea with your father earlier."

"How about a nice hearty breakfast?" Sam suggested. He started pulling eggs, bacon, and butter from the refrigerator. "With two of my very special ladies.

Trista couldn't help but feel love for her Dad. And she knew then everything was going to be okay.

Chapter Twenty-Six

Little Palm Island was everything Trista imagined. And more. The only way to get to the five-acre island was by boat or seaplane. It was situated a few miles offshore near Marathon in the Florida Keys. They parked in a designated parking lot for the boat transportation to the private island. After checking in with guest services, the hostess met them with Gumby Slumber drinks, the island's specialty cocktail. Riker and Trista took their drinks and boarded *The Truman*, the water shuttle to the island. During the ten-minute boat ride, Riker took Trista's hand in his own.

"What did you think about The Bar?"

Trista thought about his question. After arriving in the Keys yesterday, Riker had taken her to his friend's bar. It wasn't anything spectacular and looked like any other bar up and down Highway 1. A large tiki hut served as the main bar area, and it overlooked the water. Several wait staff delivered tropical concoctions to guests who wished to dig their feet in the sand and watch the sunset. Despite its lack of originality, the bar was packed with locals and tourists alike. After meeting Riker's friend and bar owner, Stan Hayes, Trista had excused herself to do some shopping while they talked business. Afterward, she and Riker packed up and headed toward Little Palm Island to spend the night.

"I thought it was a nice place. The tourists seemed to love it," Trista answered honestly.

"According to the figures Stan gave me, this place pulls in close to six figures a year."

"What about expenses? Hurricane insurance? Employee benefits?"

"After expenses, The Bar clears about forty-five grand a year."

"Not bad," Trista thought. It was hard enough for restaurants and bars to break even much less make a profit. Although living in the Keys could be expensive, pulling in forty-five grand a year wasn't too bad.

"You can swing that?" Trista asked delicately. She never had any discussions with Riker about money or finances. She assumed he lived on his bartending income and odd jobs doing construction work. Money differences never bothered her. It was important to her to make her own way in life, and she had always worked hard and saved her money. The last thing she wanted to do was have to depend on someone else to take care of her.

"I have some of my own investments. Remember Club Aqua?"

"You own it?"

Riker shrugged. "I'm part owner. Twenty-five percent."

"I had no idea. What else don't I know about you?"

"I have a few real estate investments and have been lucky in the stock market. The money I make at the bar is only spending money. I own my house outright. I can make this happen." Riker took her hand in his. "We can find a place in Key Largo. It's only a short drive to Miami for you if you have to get to the airport and, for me, a short drive to The Bar."

Trista stared out at the rushing, white water that was the boat's wake. She had no idea Riker had that kind of money. Of course, it didn't change the way she thought about him. Rich, poor, it didn't matter. She was falling in love with him. "Let's enjoy our time at the resort. We can talk about everything when we get home. I want to *not* think for the whole day."

Riker kissed her on the cheek. "Okay. No more talk about work or money. Let's enjoy each other."

The dock master and an island hostess met them when they stepped off the boat and into paradise. The island hostess introduced herself as Mila, and she escorted them to their private bungalow. On the way, they passed the island's restaurant, a tropical pool complete with waterfall, the health spa, a human-sized checkerboard game displayed in the sand, and the Zen garden, which had a koi pond, a bridge, and gazebo.

Trista immediately felt the stress of the last few weeks leave her body as they explored the private island. Finally they arrived at their own little thatched-roof bungalow. Walking inside, Trista took in the cozy living area decorated with a Tommy Bahama theme. A dozen roses, a bottle of chilled champagne, and a tray of chocolate-covered strawberries greeted them on the coffee table. The bedroom held a king-sized bed with romantic netting draped overhead. Tropical-scented candles lit up the room. A bathroom with a claw-foot tub, two separate sinks, and an entrance to the outdoor shower completed the ensemble.

"I think I'm in heaven," Trista gushed to Riker as he held her hand tightly.

The bellboy came inside and set their luggage down on the floor. "Dinner is served from six to eleven. The spa is open from nine to six.

We have all kinds of water sports and fishing. Go see the guide at the kayak stand behind the pool. Anything else?" she asked.

Riker handed a tip to Mila and the bellboy. "We're all set. Thank you." He closed the door behind them and took Trista in his arms. "Get naked," he demanded, before kissing her.

Trista could see his erection straining against the fabric of his jeans. Just seeing him excited made her feel the same way. She eased her dress over her head then slipped off her panties, standing before him naked. He did the same, stepping out of his jeans and underwear and then unbuttoning his shirt. He took her hand and led her over to the couch, where he sat down, pulling her toward him.

"Show me how much you want me," Riker said.

Trista licked her lips as she eased herself over Riker. She took his thick cock in her hand, moving the head back and forth over her opening, teasing him mercilessly.

"Good God! You're so fucking wet. I want to taste your sweetness," Riker growled.

Leaning forward, Trista sank down hard on the entire length of his cock. She sat still for a moment, clenching her muscles.

"Holy shit, babe." He grabbed a handful of her hair, as she plunged her tongue in his mouth. She lifted her hips, sinking down on him again, harder and harder. His other hand slipped under her bottom, guiding her up and down as she continued to ride him.

"I love the way you feel when you are inside of me." Trista gripped his shoulder as she continued to grind against him.

"I'm going to come," Riker moaned as the sensation built for both of them.

"Riker!" She called out his name as she reached a climax of epic proportions. She collapsed on top of him, feeling him shudder beneath her.

"I'd say now is a good time to test the outdoor shower," he panted in her ear.

***

The next morning, Trista woke to the smell of fresh coffee. She opened her eyes to find she was alone in the cavernous king bed. Her hand felt the warm indention in the covers where Riker had slept beside her all night. Wrapping her nude body in a luxurious robe the resort had graciously provided, she wandered into the living area looking for Riker. The room was empty. She opened the front door of the cottage to find him on the front porch. Dressed in boxer shorts—and nothing else—he had an apple in one hand and a knife in the other. She watched as he cut off pieces of the apple and then threw them one by one into the bushes. The sun was beginning to rise over the Atlantic Ocean.

"What in the world are you doing?" she asked him. He smiled and whispered, "Shhhh. You have to come see this baby."

Suddenly interested in whatever had her boyfriend all excited about an apple, she walked quietly to his side. Miniature deer, three of them, were standing below the porch, happily munching on the apple slices. The deer were so close she could've reached down and touched them.

"Aren't these the cutest things you've ever seen?" Riker said quietly, throwing out another piece of apple. "The maintenance guy came by here earlier and told me the Key deer swim over to the island in the middle of night to forage for food. Usually they swim back over to their side of the island by sunrise. As you can see, they're a little shy."

Trista wrapped her arms around Riker's waist as she watched him feed the deer. Yes, they were cute. And so was her boyfriend. "Who are you? And what did you do with my boyfriend?"

"Hey, I have a sensitive side too." He tossed the last of the apple slices and then the core. The smallest of the three tucked the whole core into its mouth. With the roar of an incoming golf cart, the Key deer scattered into the bushes. One of the maintenance men waved as he drove by.

"They sure do get started early in the morning," Trista commented as she watched the golf cart zoom by.

"I imagine it takes a lot of people to run this island."

"Hmmmm. I hate we have to go back tomorrow." Trista laid her head against his chest.

"I have a special surprise for you." He tucked a loose tendril of Trista's hair behind her ear. "How does some time at the spa sound?"

"Sounds about as delicious as you," she teased, reaching up to nibble on his ear.

"I booked you a half day at the spa starting at ten o'clock this morning."

"Ahhh. I see. Sending me to the spa is a ruse so you can spend the day fishing?"

He laughed. "You're on to me. Just a few hours of flats fishing. There's a guide who the island recommends, and he guarantees a fun time."

"I can guarantee a fun time if you stay here with me." She licked her lips and ran her hand down his chest.

"Very tempting." He gave her butt a hearty slap. "Seriously, I realized something."

"What is that?"

"We've never been on a proper date."

Trista thought about it for a moment. "I do have a bad habit of doing things back-ass backwards. Sex first, then dating."

"After your spa day, I'd like to take you to dinner. Consider it our first date."

"Do I have to put out?"

Riker laughed. "It's optional."

"Go on, do your fishing thing. We can meet back at the cottage for a little rendezvous before dinner?"

"Deal."

While Riker took off for his fishing trip, Trista had a few minutes to kill before her first spa appointment. She snuck her cell phone out of her luggage and put it in her pocket. She had seen all the signs around the island regarding cell phones: a red circle with an angry red slash through it and the wording NO CELL PHONES ALLOWED. There were also no TV's in the bungalows or on the island, except for one flat-screen TV in the library was used during football season. Apparently you couldn't keep the men away from their sports. She understood the idea of "it's an island and time for rest and relaxation…leave your worries and cell phones behind" but Trista had seen other people sneaking calls on their cell phones. She desperately needed to check her messages and see if Kate had called.

Walking around the island to search for a private spot, she found the Zen garden. It was used for meditations and massage therapy sessions, and was a great place for photographs. They even held small weddings there. If she ever got engaged again, this place, she thought, would be the perfect place for a wedding. Looking around, she saw the garden was empty, save for a few egrets that were eyeing fish in the koi pond.

She turned on her cell phone, not expecting to get much of a signal. To her surprise, she had full bars and a 4G connection. Quickly checking her voicemail, she had several urgent messages from Kate: call ASAP. And she had a message from Quinn, asking how things were going. Trista realized she hadn't spoken to Quinn since she found out about Blake's marriage—and her new replacement on the show. Waiting for Kate to pick up her call, she nervously paced back and forth.

"Congratulations, kid. You got the job!" Kate greeted her after the fourth ring.

"Are you serious?" Trista yelled out, scaring away the egrets.

"They want you in New York on Friday to sign the contract. Rehearsals start a few weeks afterward."

Trista started to say okay before she realized the big play for Blue Mountain Beach Children's Theatre was on Saturday night, with a matinee on Sunday. She couldn't miss it and let down all the children she had been working with for weeks.

"I can't make it Friday. I have obligations this weekend."

"Trista..." Katie started.

"I'm sorry. I just can't." Trista dug her heel in the sand. "Why can't they send me the contract to sign via email?"

"They can, but the director has a cast meeting set up for Friday morning. I figured we could do everything then."

"How long do you think the meeting will last?"

Katie sighed. "You never know. A couple hours maybe?"

Trista mentally calculated flight times in her head. If she left tomorrow morning, she could fly out of Miami directly to New York. She would be there bright and early for the cast meetings. Sign the contract. And fly back to Blue Mountain Beach in time for dress rehearsal at six. At the very least, she would miss dress rehearsal, but she would be there for opening night and the matinee on Sunday. She could fly out again later in the week to start apartment hunting so she would be settled by the time rehearsals started. She would tell Riker about the new job tonight at dinner. They could still see each on weekends. It could work.

"Trista, are you still there? Is everything okay?"

"I can be there by tomorrow night. I have to leave by Friday afternoon and come back for the weekend. Like I said, I have obligations this weekend I can't get out of." Trista told Kate about the play and her role as director.

"I understand. Just make it work."

"Okay. See ya tomorrow!"

Chapter Twenty-Seven

"You look beautiful," Riker said as Trista walked out of the bathroom. After a half day of spa treatments, including a body scrub and heavenly massage with ginger and mango oils, she glowed from head to toe. She wore her favorite maxi dress, a simple, white chiffon dress with a plunging neckline and a glittering, sequin gold band around the waist. The dress reminded her of something a Greek goddess would wear. All she needed were the olive branches in her hair for decoration. She pulled her hair into a loose bun with several tendrils framing her heart shaped face. A swipe of lip-gloss, a touch of blush, and a coat of mascara were her only makeup. Her tanned skin glistened from her favorite vanilla-scented body lotion.

"Thank you," Trista said twirling around for a dramatic effect. "A day at the spa was what I needed." She kissed him on the cheek. "You look ravishing too."

"I clean up pretty well." Riker was wearing pressed khaki slacks and a black polo shirt. His dark hair hit a few inches below the collar and was still wet from the shower. The crystal blue color of his eyes really stood out against his tan and dark shirt he wore. He was so handsome it took Trista's breath away. She gave him a hug, relishing the way he smelled of her favorite men's cologne, Bulgari. "You better stop or we won't be on time for our dinner reservations," he teased.

She could feel him hardening against her thigh as she giggled and took a step back. "I think we should take our desserts back to the room after dinner."

"Great idea," he agreed with a wink.

Dinner was a five-course affair with crab-cake appetizers, coconut lobster bisque, grilled swordfish and mango salsa for her, coriander-crusted elk for him, and key lime pie and chocolate Kahlua cake to-go. During their dinner, Trista wanted to bring up the play in New York but couldn't bring herself to do it, yet. She settled on waiting until they went back to the cottage.

They paid the check and headed back. "I'm going to need a workout after all this delicious food," Trista said, opening the door. Riker had secretly arranged for turndown service. The housekeeper had already come by and lit candles all throughout the cottage. Rose petals were scattered over the bed and around the floor. A bottle of champagne was chilling in the ice bucket.

She gasped with appreciation. "Wow, I'm beginning to think I'm never going to leave this place." She set down the Styrofoam containers that held their desserts and picked up the champagne. "Dom?"

"I say we get started now with a little warm-up." He took away the chilled bottle of Dom and pulled Trista into his arms, kissing her.

Trista tried to pull away. It was now or never. She couldn't keep putting off telling Riker about New York. "I have something I want to talk to you about."

He held her tightly with one arm and used his other hand to work the zipper on her dress. "No talking. It can wait."

"No, it can't wait. I need to—"

Riker covered her mouth with his. His tongue hungrily explored her mouth. While he kissed her, he carried her to the bed. Staring at her nude body in the candlelight, he whispered, “Wow. You look amazing.”

Trista started to speak again, but realized it was useless. Once Riker got into sex mode, nothing could stray him. He stepped out of his clothes and got into bed with her. “Let’s make this a night to remember,” he said, running his hands down her body. Trista closed her eyes as his mouth sucked on her nipple and his fingers found her wet and ready for him. After two hours of delicious love- making, and three intense and memorable orgasms, she felt herself drift off.

At midnight, Trista woke up thirsty. She looked over at Riker, who was softly snoring, his sexy, nude body half-covered with a tangled sheet. She tiptoed into the bathroom and filled a glass with tap water. Her throat was parched; she greedily drank the water in one long gulp. Returning to the bedroom, she found Riker awake, sitting up in bed.

“What’s wrong?” he asked.

“Just thirsty. Sorry, I didn’t mean to wake you.”

He patted the bed, and she sat down next him. Stroking her hair, he said, “I can tell when you’ve got something going on in that pretty head of yours. What’s up?”

“We do need to talk.” Trista pulled the covers over her body.

“Okay.” He sat up straighter. “If this is about your sister. I’d like to talk to her—”

She interrupted him. “It’s not about that. I am moving to New York.”

“What? When?”

Taking a deep breath, she continued. “I got a job offer to star in a leading role for *Love Potion #9*. It’s an opportunity of a lifetime. The play starts rehearsals soon, and then we're slated to do a six-month run on Broadway."

"When do you leave?"

"Next week."

"How… *when* did all this happen?"

Trista told him about the call from her agent. The quick trip to New York to read for the director. And the call she'd received from her agent telling her the good news this morning.

"So you've known all this time there could be a possibility of a job waiting for you in New York? While we were in Key West and I was making plans for us to move here?"

"Wait a minute. I never agreed to a move to Key West. I only said I would accompany you to take a look at the bar."

"Yeah, well you never said *anything* about New York."

"I wasn't sure it was even going to happen until today. I didn't want to say anything until I was sure."

"So you're taking the job?" Riker studied her face.

She nodded slowly.

"I guess there's nothing else to talk about then." He jumped off the bed and pulled his suitcase open. He pulled on a pair of shorts and a t-shirt then started to throw the clothes he'd worn to dinner in the bag.

Trista tried to touch him on the arm, but he pulled away from her. She said, "I don't understand why you're so upset. We can still see each other."

"When?"

She started to say, "On the weekends," but she realized this job would be a full-time commitment. Daily rehearsals with evening performances. Weekends were not an option. This would be a six- or seven-day-a-week job with little time off until the play closed or she moved on to something else.

"You knew I was looking for other work. This situation has always been temporary."

"Which situation? You and I?"

"I meant me living in Florida. It was never a permanent thing."

"You never told me that."

"You never asked."

Riker slammed his suitcase shut. "Then I guess there is nothing left to talk about. It seems you've made up your mind."

Trista watched as Riker grabbed his toiletry bag and headed for the bathroom. "Can you please quit packing and sit down and talk to me?"

Riker kept walking to the bathroom. "There is nothing left to say. It sounds like you've made up your mind. Commuting to and from New York is out of the question." He turned when he got to the door and stared at her. "It's over Trista." He slammed the bathroom door shut.

Trista sat on the couch, stunned. This was her career. Her life. Why she should give up her dreams?

***

The next morning Trista woke up before sunrise. Riker was still asleep. After their argument, he spent the next two hours on the front deck drinking beer. She pretended like she was asleep when he came back inside, drunk and stumbling into furniture. She was already packed and ready to go. She had arranged for a private car to drive her to the Miami airport. The chauffeured ride had cost her a pretty penny, but it was worth it. The last thing she wanted to do was ask Riker to drive her. She knew his plane didn't leave until three in the afternoon. She hastily wrote him a note on the Little Palm Island stationery.

Riker,
I booked a flight out of Miami to New York for eight thirty this morning. I wish things had turned out differently. My feelings for you are strong, but you know it's important to me to put my career back on track. I hope you'll understand why I had to go.
Love,
Trista

She left the note on her side of the bed, where Riker would see it when he woke up. With tears in her eyes, she kissed him gently on the forehead and left him sleeping. She put her overnight bag on her shoulder and left the cottage. Walking down the steps of the bungalow, she saw the Key deer waiting by the porch, hoping for more apples. She smiled, remembering Riker throwing the fruit to the deer. Walking down the path to the dock and her waiting boat, she thought about the great time she had spent here with Riker. But she never looked back.

Chapter Twenty-Eight

"Trista, you better hurry up if you're going to make curtain call!" Nicolette yelled through the intercom system.

Trista was in her room putting on the finishing touches of her makeup. She had just flown in from New York. Unfortunately, she didn't make it in time for dress rehearsals, but she had called Michelle and explained her situation. "No problem. I can cover for you. Please get home in time for opening night!" Michelle had told her over the phone. "And congratulations on the new job!"

Trista was nervous about seeing Riker again. He hadn't called her since she left him in the Keys. When she got home last night, she told her family about the job in New York. Her father was happy. Nicolette seemed to be truly happy for her. Everyone was happy for her it seemed...except Riker.

Putting on a pair of her favorite gold hoops, Trista stood at the French doors and watched the quiet surf. She realized, as much as she loved the city, she was going to miss the peace and calm of living at the beach. And seeing Riker. She wished things had turned out differently. Even though they weren't seeing each other anymore, she still needed to tell Nicolette about their relationship. She wanted to clear the air with her sister and try to start fresh before she moved to New York.

After tonight's performance, she planned on doing that. No more excuses.

It was a full house at the Blue Mountain Beach Children's Theatre. Trista escorted her father, Madeline, and Nicolette to the front row before she went backstage to meet with the kids. There was a nervous excitement backstage and complete pandemonium. Kids were running everywhere, some dressed in their costumes, other frantically putting on their costumes, and some going over their lines again. Trista found Michelle, who was talking to Amelia, one of the lead characters in the play. Already dressed in costume, Amelia was blowing her nose with a tissue.

"Amelia, are you okay?" Trista asked, looking at the child with concern.

"Amelia thinks she's coming down with a sinus infection and sore throat," Michelle answered for her.

"I'm a little hoarse," Amelia said. She looked cute with her blue gingham dress and brown hair in braided pigtails. A smattering of freckles dotted her nose and the top of her cheeks. Amelia reminded Trista of herself when she was that age. When she was ten, Trista was the lead in *Cat in the Hat*. She had a bad stomach bug the night before the play opened. She could've stayed home and let her understudy do her part. Instead she filled up on the pink liquid stuff and performed in the play.

"Do you feel like going on tonight?" Trista asked her.

Amelia nodded.

"Great. How about some hot tea to soothe your throat? Tea always helps me when I have a sore throat." Trista grabbed Michelle by the arm and headed to the back of the stage where there were dressing rooms and a small kitchen. She put a mug of water in the microwave and pushed a button to start it.

"We go on in thirty minutes." Michelle plucked a teabag from a box of Celestial Seasonings. "All we have is chamomile."

"That's fine." Trista removed the mug from the microwave and put the teabag inside.

"What's going on with you and Riker?" Michelle asked. "I mean, I know it's none of my business but—"

Trista froze in place. "How did you know about me and Riker?"

"It's pretty obvious, Trista." Michelle stirred the teabag around in the mug. "Like I said, I know it's none of my business, but I can't stand to see anyone get hurt."

"What do you mean?"

"I've known Riker a long time. He's been volunteering at the theatre for three years. I've never seen him unhappy. For the last two days, he's been sulking. He hasn't been himself. Usually you guys are inseparable around here. I haven't seen you say two words to him tonight." She handed the mug to Trista. "It's about New York?"

Trista nodded. "He doesn't want me to take the job."

"I doubt that. I don't think Riker would want you to hold anything back because of him."

Trista thought about it for a moment. "I didn't tell him about the job until after I decided to take it." She told Michelle about her secret trip to New York. "Riker and I went to the Keys this past week, and I finally told him what was going on. He didn't take it too well."

"If I know Riker as well as I think I do, he is probably upset you kept it from him. More than he is that you took the job. Do you love him?"

"Yes," Trista answered quickly. "I do."

"Then you need to tell him. Nothing gets in the way of true love. Not even two thousand miles. You can make it work."

Trista grabbed a paper towel and wrapped it around the mug. "Thanks, Michelle."

"Now let's get out there and give our audience a great show!"

As they walked out of the kitchen, Nicolette was standing in the hallway. Trista bumped into her and splashed some tea onto the tiled floor. "Nicolette! I'm so sorry. I didn't see you standing there."

"I was only coming by to wish you good luck."

Trista wondered how long Nicolette had been standing outside the kitchen. How much did she hear?

"It doesn't seem like you need any luck though," Nicolette continued. "How long, Trista?"

Michelle looked over at Trista with a surprised look on her face. She took the mug out of her hands. "I'll take this over to Amelia."

"I can't talk about this right now. After the show." Trista tried to walk away, but Nicolette grabbed her arm, digging her nails into her skin.

"I want to know right now! How long have you been sleeping with my boyfriend?" Nicolette's voice grew louder as she spoke. Once she got mad, it was hard to get her to calm down. Two boys were playing in the hallway, and they both stopped and stared at the two sisters.

"Oww," Trista whispered. "You're hurting me."

"I can't believe I didn't figure this out sooner," Nicolette continued, keeping her grip tight. "I knew something wasn't right, but I didn't see it."

"Nicolette, keep your voice down. It's not what you think." Trista was able to finally wretch her arm away from her sister just in time. Angry red marks were slashed on her forearm.

Nicolette pursed her lips together in thought. She started to pace back and forth in the tight hallway. "The other night when we went to the Liars Club. Riker fixed you a drink without asking what you wanted. How did he know you liked margaritas on the rocks? No salt? Then Crazy Jack said he remembered you from the other night. That was the first night you had come in town. Did you fuck my boyfriend then? Or was it the night of his surprise party? I saw you two walking up from the beach. You were walking very close to one another. In deep conversation about something. You both tracked a lot of sand into the house. Did you fuck him that night too? After you both started volunteering at the theatre. Lots of late nights together. Let's not forget your attempts at setting me up with other men, like Brent, so you could have Riker to yourself." Nicolette's tone continued to rise with each accusation. People began to walk toward them to see what the commotion was about.

"Please lower your voice. We can't talk about this here," Trista said through gritted teeth.

"Tell me the truth," Nicolette persisted. She stopped pacing and stood right in Trista's face.

"We met the first night I came back to Florida." Trista clenched her fists, her fingernails cutting into her palms. "I didn't know you two were dating. I swear. And when I found out you two knew each other…the night of the surprise party, Riker told me you were not a couple anymore."

"I can't believe this! So you *were* with Riker before the party?" Nicolette's face turned bright red.

"Like I said, it was a random thing. I stopped by the Liar's Club on my way into town. He needed a ride home. One thing led to another."

"You're a fucking whore," Nicolette hissed.

“Nicolette, please.” Trista turned to the kids who had gathered behind Nicolette and told them to go back to the stage. She turned her attention back to her sister. “It wasn’t like that. I just…”

Nicolette slapped Trista across the face. “You are not my sister! Sisters don’t betray each other like this! You’re dead to me!” She turned and stomped down the hallway.

Trista was trembling by the time she made it to the stage. Riker was talking to Michelle, and they both turned as she walked by. He started to come to her, but Trista waved him off. She rubbed her cheek, which she knew had a huge red handprint across it, and put a smile on her face. *As the saying goes, the show must go on.* Pushing Nicolette’s accusations out of her mind, she addressed everyone.

“Listen up!” Trista gathered everyone in a large circle. “This is it! Everything we’ve worked hard for these last few weeks. Remember your lines. If you forget anything, keep the dialogue going like we rehearsed. Help each other out when you can. Most of all, let’s have fun!”

“Okay, places everyone!” Michelle said. “We go on in two minutes!” She shot Trista a concerned look.

Trista smiled brightly and gave Michelle a thumbs-up. She stepped off stage when the house lights started to flash off and on, signaling to the audience the play was about to begin. She took a deep cleansing breath and said a little prayer. The curtain rose slowly. From her position at the back of the stage, she could see where her father and Madeline sat. Beside Madeline was an empty chair, where Nicolette should be. For the rest of the night, the chair was vacant.

Chapter Twenty-Nine

The after party was held at Blue Crush, a restaurant and wine bar adjacent to the theatre. A special kids buffet table was set up with mac-n-cheese, chicken tenders, hamburger sliders, cookies, and an ice cream bar. For the adults, waiters passed around heavy hors d'oeuvre and champagne.

Trista wanted to talk to Riker and warn him about Nicolette, but she couldn't get away from the crowd of people. Every child's parent had come up to her and congratulated her on the success of the play. It seemed all of the locals who lived in and around Blue Mountain Beach had turned out for the production. And they all wanted to talk to Trista.

Michelle had pulled her aside and told her this was the most successful play the theatre had every done. "In ten years of its existence we have never made this much money. We had a full house tonight and tomorrow's matinee is also sold out. Donations were through the roof! We've raised over three hundred thousand dollars!" Michelle was ecstatic. "Do you know what that will pay for? New costumes, materials for the sets, a field trip to New York for the kids!"

"I'm glad I could be a part of it," Trista said sincerely.

"I know you were offered the job in New York, but we would love to have you next year. If you're free."

"We'll see about that." Trista gave her a smile. "I promise." She looked around the crowded restaurant for Riker. She almost gave up when she spotted him at the bar, talking to another guy who'd helped with the sets. "Excuse me, Michelle. I'll be back in a minute."

Michelle followed her gaze to the bar. She gave Trista a pat on the back. "Good luck, hon."

Trista weaved her way through the crowd, occasionally stopping to say hello to people who grabbed her arm. She stopped for photographs and signed autographs. By the time she reached the bar, Riker was gone.

"Hey, Gary," Trista said, approaching the guy Riker had been talking to. "Great job tonight."

"Thank you." Gary downed whatever he was drinking. "Can I get you a drink?"

"Actually, I was looking for Riker. Do you know where he went?"

"Men's room, I think."

Trista thanked him and then headed toward the men's room. She wanted to catch him before he left. After tomorrow's matinee, she had a flight to New York, and there wouldn't be another time to say goodbye. She hated the way she'd left things with him. As soon as she spotted him coming out the bathroom, she grabbed his arm. "Let's talk."

"I don't think there's anything left to say." Riker pulled away, putting his hands in his jeans pockets.

"Please."

"All right. But not in here. Let's walk outside."

Trista followed him outside. He led her across the street to the pathway down the beach. Taking off their shoes, they plunged into the soft, white sand. A group of teenagers were having a bonfire, all gathered around a guy playing a guitar. Riker led Trista in the opposite direction toward a group of sand dunes. They sat down at the edge of the dunes.

"I'm sorry," Trista started. "I know I shouldn't have lied to you about New York. I really didn't think I would get the job. I know it's no excuse, but I wasn't ready to tell anyone. I thought I would fly up there, read for the part, and come back home. I wasn't expecting anything to come out of it."

"Is this what you want, Trista? You want to live in New York?"

She looked at the moon and the cloudless sky, stars sparkling brightly like diamonds. The reflection of the moon hit the water like it was shining a path to the end of the world.

"I think I do. I realized when I went up there how much I really missed the place. The energy. The fast pace. The excitement. Most of all, I realized I missed working on a stage. A real Broadway stage. The live performances. Everything."

Riker brought his knees up and rested his elbows on them. "I could see that tonight. The way you were with the kids. The excitement in your eyes during the play. You really enjoy doing this."

"I do. I really do."

He put her hand in his and squeezed. "I love you, Trista Carmichael. I want you to be happy."

"Would you go to New York with me?" She loved the way Riker's strong hand held hers. "I know you love the beach as much as I love the city. And I know how much you want to buy The Bar, but—"

"I love you more than The Bar." He leaned over and kissed her on the cheek. "I might be willing to give New York a try."

She scooted over until she was practically sitting in his lap. She nuzzled her head on his shoulders. "I love you, James Riker."

"What about your sister? We can't put off telling her anymore."

"She already knows." Trista told him about the argument she had with Nicolette before the play.

"I knew something must've gone wrong when I saw Nic practically run off the stage. I'm sorry I wasn't with you when it happened," Riker said.

Trista thought back to her conversation with her father. "I can't keep worrying about my sister and what she thinks of me. I have to live my own life."

"Where is she now?"

"I don't think she stuck around for the play. Her seat was empty the entire the time."

Riker checked his watch. "It's getting late. Let's go say our goodbyes at the restaurant. Then we can go back to your place."

"My dad and Madeline are at the house. They went straight home after the play was over. I think Dad was worried about Nicolette."

"Then my place it is." He helped her up. "At least we'll have one night together before you leave."

Chapter Thirty

"Last night ended in a way I would've never expected," Trista said, snuggling with Riker.

"Why do you say that?"

"I didn't think you were ever going to speak to me again."

"It was a lonely trip back from the Keys. I realized as soon as I woke up and found your note that I couldn't let you leave Blue Mountain Beach without me. I wasn't sure if you wanted me back."

Trista smiled. "Do you think you'll like living in a big city?"

"I've been to New York before, but I never imagined myself living in a big city. But then again, I never thought I would hook up with a movie star either!"

Trista laughed and punched him on the arm. "Hook up, huh?"

"Best hook up in my life."

"I bet."

"Now I need to figure out what the hell I'm going to do for job."

"There are a lot of bars in the city."

"I wasn't thinking of bartending."

"What else? Construction?"

"I really enjoyed working with the children's theatre. Maybe I can find something similar?" He shrugged.

She lifted her head off the pillow. “Actually that’s a great idea. I’m sure I can help find you something.”

“What time is your flight again?” He looked at the alarm clock resting on his nightstand. “It’s almost six now.”

“I’m catching the last plane out. Not until eight tonight.”

“I’ll let you get settled before I come up for my first visit. Then I’m going to have to work through spring and get someone else trained before summer.” Riker caressed her face. “Until it’s all settled, I’ll come for lots of visits.”

Trista reached for her cell phone, realizing the battery had died sometime in the middle of the night. “Mind if I use your charger?” She plugged in her iPhone and waited for it to charge up.

“I’ll make us some coffee.” Riker got out of bed. “And breakfast. Then we can go back to your place if you’d like some help packing. We have time before today’s matinee.”

“That sounds wonderful. I told Dad I would spend the rest of the day with him before I left.”

“Is he going to be sticking around for a while?”

“I think so. He’s planning on handing over the company reins to Nicolette. Afterward, he and Madeline will probably start cruising the world again.”

“I’m sure that’ll be good for him,” he said and headed toward the kitchen.

Trista used the bathroom to freshen up. She splashed cool water on her face and did the toothpaste-and-finger routine to brush the yuckies from her mouth. Just as she was pulling her hair back into a ponytail, she heard the familiar pings of her voicemail. She realized she hadn’t called Quinn back yet. The message was probably from her.

Picking up her phone, she noticed several missed calls and texts from her father last night—all before her phone had died. She read the first one, her body filling with icy dread.

CALL ME ASAP. NICOLETTE IN AN ACCIDENT.

TRISTA CALL US. MADELINE.

CALL IMMEDIATELY.

Trista grabbed her purse and headed for the front door. "I gotta go!" she shouted as she passed by the kitchen. Riker was standing at the coffee pot pouring the caffeinated liquid into mugs.

"Wait! Trista! What's wrong?" He dropped the mugs and ran to the front door.

"It's Nicolette. She's been in an accident." Trista put the phone up to her ear and waited for her dad to answer.

"Wait! Don't go anywhere. I'll drive you. Just give me a sec to throw on some pants." Riker sprinted to his room.

The call went straight to voicemail. Trista hung up and redialed. She cursed when it happened again. "Hurry!" she shouted from the door.

Thirty seconds later, Riker was in her car driving them to the hospital. Trista called Our Sacred Lady Hospital and asked the receptionist if her sister had been admitted. While she waited for an answer, Riker drove quickly through the deserted streets. "If she was in an accident, that's where she would be," Riker told her. "It's the only hospital in the area that has an ER and a trauma center."

Trista heart pounded, and she felt like she was going to come out of her skin. She wondered what had happened to her sister.

Finally her dad's call beeped in while she was waiting for the hospital receptionist to come back on the line. "Dad!" she answered the call.

"Nicolette was in an accident. She's in ICU at Our Sacred Lady. Do you know where that is?" Sam asked breathlessly.

"Of course. We're on the way! What happened?"

"We don't know all the details yet. She was driving near Inlet Beach, and her car went off the road and crashed into a parked car." Her dad paused for a second. "Trista, they don't think she's going to make it."

Riker pulled into the hospital parking lot as she got off the phone with her dad. He dropped her off at the main entrance. She ran inside the hospital lobby and to the elevators. Madeline met her at the third-floor nurse's station.

Madeline hugged her and said, "I'm so sorry, baby. Your sister is hanging in there." She led Trista down the corridor to a waiting area.

"Can I see her?" Trista asked. A lump had formed in her throat, making it difficult for her to speak.

"She's in ICU, honey. They aren't allowing anyone back there right now." They stopped outside the locked doors and pushed a buzzer. "We have to wait for a nurse to let us back in." A couple minutes later, a nurse who was familiar with Madeline let them in. They walked to a room labeled FAMILY WAITING AREA. It was a spacious room with several leather lounge chairs and recliners. There was only one other family in the room, and they were huddled by a coffeemaker. An older woman with the group was sobbing uncontrollably while the others comforted her.

Sam was pacing by the vending machines. When he saw Trista, he rushed toward her. Trista hugged her father. "Dad, what happened?"

"They think she might've fallen asleep at the wheel. She was going pretty fast when she hit the parked car."

"When did this happen?"

"Around midnight. A tourist found the car and called 9-1-1."

"Can I see her?"

"Not yet. The doctors are with her now. She has severe head trauma. Swelling of the brain. The doctors aren't very optimistic right now."

"They don't know Nicolette," Trista said.

Her father smiled weakly. "You're right. He doesn't know she's made of steel. Where's Riker?"

Trista said, "Crap. I forgot. He dropped me off before he parked the car. Madeline, can you go get him?"

She nodded and headed back downstairs.

As soon as she left, a doctor stood in the doorway. "Mr. Ricci?" he called out as he walked toward them.

"This is my other daughter, Trista," Sam introduced the two.

If the doctor recognized Trista, he didn't say anything. He nodded and continued, "Nicolette is heavily sedated. Her most recent CT scan still shows significant swelling of the brain. We need to keep her as comfortable as possible."

"How long will she need to be sedated?" Sam asked.

The doctor looked between him and Trista. "With the type of injuries Nicolette has sustained, there's really no telling. I'm sorry I can't be more precise. Brain injuries are tricky. Some people pull out of it quickly with no subsequent problems, while others…they never fully recover. I wish I had better news."

"Does she have any other injuries?" Trista asked. "I mean, other than the brain swelling?"

"Nothing life threatening. A couple of broken fingers and minor burns, likely from when the airbag deployed. The swelling is our only concern right now." The doctor patted Trista on the arm before shaking Sam's hand. "We'll take good care of Nicolette. The nurses will escort you to see her for a few minutes. Remember, though, she needs her rest. Family visits only for now."

Trista followed her dad to the ICU nurse's station. Protocol demanded they wash their hands and put on antibacterial gel before entering Nicolette's room. There was a nurse standing next to Nicolette's bed, changing out one of the IV bags. Before she left, the nurse said to them, "Some doctors think people who are in comas can hear what people are saying around them. Positive thoughts and messages can go a long way." She smiled and left them alone with Nicolette.

Sam grabbed Trista's hand, and warned her. "She's wrapped in a lot of bandages. Nicolette doesn't look like herself."

Trista squeezed his hand. "It's okay, Dad."

Despite her father's warning, Trista let out a small gasp at the sight of her sister. Tubes and wires snaked in and around Nicolette's body. Her face—what little could be seen—was covered with angry purple bruises. There was a white bandage surrounding the top of her head. An IV pump had three bags of different meds slowly dripping into her sister's fragile body.

Trista reached out and gently took her sister's hand in her own. She looked at her dad, who was standing on the other side of the bed, with uncertainty.

"Go ahead, honey. She needs to hear encouraging words from us." Sam gently pushed her toward the hospital bed, saying in Italian, "Dille che ama (*Tell her you love her*)."

For once, Trista was at a loss for words. She blew out a breath before beginning. "Hey, Nicolette. It's me, Trista. I want you to know I love you, and I need you to get better. I know we've had our differences, but I don't know what I'd do without you. You're strong, and I know you'll pull through this." Trista couldn't help the tears that started to fall freely down her face. "Cuz if you don't wake up soon I'm going to have to furnish and decorate your new house all by myself. And I know how much you hate my sense of style." She leaned over and kissed her sister on the one bare spot on her cheek that wasn't covered in bandages.

Trista then stood by the window while her father whispered a few things in Nicolette's ear. The same nurse came by and told them time was up. When they got back to the waiting room, Madeline was back with Riker. Trista fell into his arms, and they hugged for what seemed like hours.

For two days, Trista stayed in the ICU waiting room with her dad, Madeline, and Riker. They took shifts eating, sleeping, and taking showers. Visits were limited to ten minutes, a few times a day. Trista used her time with Nicolette to read to her the daily real estate reports, which she knew her sister read faithfully every morning, and telling her to get her ass out of bed and get better. The rest of the time Trista silently blamed herself for Nicolette's accident. She went over the last conversation she'd had with Nicolette at the children's theatre and how her relationship with Riker may have ruined any chance of reconciliation with her sister. Trista kept these thoughts to herself, and every time Riker tried to talk to her about it, she shut him out. Until one morning something inside of her just broke.

"I can't keep going like this, Riker." Trista pushed scrambled eggs around the plate with her plastic spork. The cafeteria food in the hospital was surprisingly good, but no one seemed to have much of an appetite.

He looked up surprised. Trista hadn't said much following her sister's accident. "What do you mean?"

"This is not going to work. I need to be here for my sister. Even if she pulls out of it, we have a long hard road ahead."

"We can do this together." Riker reached for her hand. "I love you and—"

Trista pulled her hand away and interrupted him. "No, we can't. I'm responsible for my sister's accident. She's in that room because of me. Because of what we did. If…when wakes up, I need to be there for her. And I can't do that if you and I are still seeing each other. " She stirred a pack of sugar into her coffee, not meeting his eye. "I'm afraid we can't do this anymore."

"Do what?" Riker asked. "Love is not like a light switch. You can't turn it on and off. Either you love me or you don't."

"I do love you, Riker. But I don't think this is the right time for us. My family needs me now. It's time we said goodbye."

He scooted his chair back, standing up. "Please don't do this."

Trista shook her head. "I'm sorry, I just can't."

Riker was silent for a few moments. "I know you need some time. I get it." He came around to her side and kissed her on the top of her head. "But know that I will always be here for you. Always."

She looked up from her coffee and watched the love of her life walk out of the hospital cafeteria.

Chapter Thirty-One

9 WEEKS LATER

Trista felt the imaginary butterflies in her stomach, as she had way back when, before her first Broadway play. Looking around her dressing room, she smiled at the abundance of flowers from well-wishers. The orchids were from her agent, the purple and yellow assorted flower basket from her father and Madeline, and three-dozen pink roses from Quinn. While she was putting on her costume, a knock at the door brought another floral delivery. This time a dozen red roses arranged in a beautiful bouquet.

"Oooh, girl, who sent these gorgeous flowers? I don't see a card," Darby said, fingering one of the stems. Darby was the makeup artist and worked exclusively for Trista. During the short six weeks she had been in New York City, they had become close, like brother and sister. She'd told Darby everything that had happened to her recently; from the time she was fired from the TV show to Blake cheating on her, to her move to Florida. "Could they be from your former lover?" he asked, referring to Riker.

Trista thought Riker was probably watching a Key West sunset right now and drinking a Mai Tai from the comfort of his new bar. She hadn't heard from him since he left her in the hospital cafeteria. It seemed like ages ago. "No, those are probably from Greg and Tony," she said of her two friends from whom she leased her new apartment.

"Honey, red is for *love*. Not gay BFFs who coordinate your outfits and help decorate your apartment."

Darby had a point. But she had made it pretty clear to Riker it was over for good. After Nicolette's accident, she felt so guilty about her relationship with him. If she had stopped sleeping with Riker from the get-go, then Nicolette would have never had her car accident. The doctors had told the family that the combination of alcohol and Valium in Nicolette's system slowed her reflexes, causing poor judgment when driving. However, Trista knew if it wasn't for her, Nicolette wouldn't have left the children's play upset and driven twice the legal speed limit down a narrow, two-lane beach highway. Nicolette had crashed into a parked car on the side of the road, totaling her own car, causing the severe brain injury. The swelling in her brain had finally subsided, and she was out of ICU within a week of the accident, and in physical rehab ten days later—all miracles. Trista considered herself lucky Nicolette had no memory of what had happened; she didn't remember the accident or any events leading up to the accident for two weeks prior. Meaning she didn't remember anything that happened between Riker and Trista. After discussing the situation with her father, they decided not to rehash the events with Nicolette until she was better. Far better. And so Trista intended to keep her promise not to see Riker again. The day Nicolette started physical rehab, Trista left for New York City at the insistence of her father. She was lucky the producer's let her keep the role, and she'd immediately started work as soon as she returned.

She put the red roses on the side table opposite of her dressing table. She situated herself in the makeup chair and waited for Darby to work his magic. "I can't think about some secret admirer sending me roses right now. I need you to make me beautiful while I go over my lines one more time," she said. She lifted her face toward the ceiling and waited.

"Honey, you're already gorgeous. And if you don't already know those lines, then you're screwed."

"Thanks for the vote of confidence."

"Thirty minutes to show time!" a voice said through an intercom system.

"I know you'll be fine." Darby finished touching up her makeup and added a spritz of body glitter. Trista stood up, twirling around in her red dress and black-sequin pumps. "You look fabulous," he added.

Trista blew him a kiss and headed out to the stage. A few minutes later, she was ready for the opening night to begin. Taking a deep breath as the curtain slowly ascended, she got a glimpse of the audience before they turned the spotlight on her. Her best friend Quinn sat in the front row, in the reserved spot Trista had arranged for her. Quinn had visited Nicolette in the hospital and helped Trista move her things to New York. She was there for her every step of the way, and for that, Trista was grateful. She was still a little disappointed her dad and Madeline couldn't make it, but she knew Nicolette needed them more right now.

Giving a small smile to Quinn, Trista focused her attention on the rest of the audience. As soon as the spotlight hit her Trista would speak the first line of the play. But a split second before the light blinded her view from the audience, she saw him. Sitting a few rows directly behind Quinn. At first she thought she was seeing things. How could she ever forget that dimpled smile, those inquisitive, blue eyes, and the way he cocked his head to the side when he was really concentrating on something? Like he was now. She blinked a few times, but she could no longer see past the front row. Her heart thudded loudly against her chest. The audience was deafeningly quiet, everyone waiting for her to speak.

All she could think about was Riker.

Author Note: To read more of Trista and Riker's story, look for the second installment of The Blue Mountain Beach series, *Sunswept*, coming soon.

About the Author

Leigha Lennox is the pen name for Traci Hohenstein, who is the #1 Amazon international bestselling author of the Rachel Scott series, which includes *Look for Me*, *Asylum Harbor*, *Burn Out*, *Cut & Run, & Deceptive Measures*. She lives in Florida with her husband and three children. Please visit tracihohensteinbooks.com or Leigha Lennox on Facebook at https://www.facebook.com/leighalennox.

Also by TRACI HOHENSTEIN

<u>Rachel Scott Series</u>

Look for Me

Asylum Harbor

Burn Out

Cut & Run

Deceptive Measures

<u>NEW from LEIGHA LENNOX – the Hollywood Hills Series</u>

Special Delivery

Split Decision

Sinfully Delicious

<u>Also from LEIGHA LENNOX – the Blue Mountain Beach Series</u>

Sunkissed

Sunswept

Made in the USA
San Bernardino, CA
30 May 2015